ii

ROUND TRIP

Shamontiel L. Vaughn

Cover Photographer: Luke M. Schierholz
http://www.inkbone.net
Publisher: Shamontiel L. Vaughn
ISBN: 978-0-6151-5615-6
Printed in the United States of America

To contact this author, visit http://www.shamontiel.com.

Got *Change for a Twenty*? Check out Shamontiel's first novel. Visit http://www.shamontiel.com for details.

About the novel:
Growing up is hard enough, but when five friends argue, cry, laugh, pledge, fight, and hang together on a historically black college campus, a bond is formed. Seleste is a college junior studying criminal justice, trying to deny her feelings for Memo, and trying to decide whether she wants to stay a virgin. Her best friend, Cara, is a college junior who lives in the dorms and has a friend with benefits, Arnez, who is more concerned with pledging with Jermaine than Arnez is with Cara. Jermaine is caught between the two because Cara is his ex-girlfriend and Arnez is in his ship. Arnez's friend, Memo, is a troubled senior from New York who came to Chicago to escape his father's past as a crooked cop. Change for a Twenty is a fiction novel set in Chicago about five college friends, two nemeses, and the path to adulthood.

Cover Art for *Change for a Twenty*: Evan J. Hunt (www.evanhuntphoto.com)

Special Thank You

I have a tattoo on my arm of a book and the words "Live to Write" around it so when a book isn't in my hands, I have a constant reminder of my means of therapy and my career. I've wanted to write novels since my elementary school editorial days with "Mr. Slick" short stories. But in 2006, I finally put that dream into effect. After much re-reading and rewriting of *Change for a Twenty*, I put my product out, and I was amazed at how many supporters I had. There are many people who were essential in helping me with my publishing goals, but two stand out the most: Mrs. Gwendolyn "Red" Y. Vaughn and Heritage Books & Music. My mother, Red, bought every single version of *Change for a Twenty* until I finally decided on one to sell to the public, read it, and gave me the constructive feedback I needed to understand the pros and the cons of my first novel, *Change for a Twenty*, as well as *Round Trip*. Forever my personal cheerleader and number one person to lean on, she trucked along with me to my very first (and most successful) book signing at Lincoln University (MO) and kept me encouraged. Sometimes I wonder if she should be a comedian because even during the most challenging book signing I've ever been involved in, she made me laugh so hard that I flew back with a smile. If I wrote it, she checked it out. If I interviewed with it, she listened. If I went, she followed. She is the definition of reliability and support and that makes me love her more each day.

The other supporter is Heritage Books & Music in Chicago. This was the first store to give my book a chance, and I couldn't have been more surprised to walk past the Granville Red Line Station headed to Subway and see *Change for a Twenty* sitting in the front window display. I jumped up and down right there in front of people driving and walking down the street. I didn't even care. I was thrilled to see it.

Thank you to all of the people who spread the word (and sales): R2C2H2 Tha Artivist of W.E.A.L.L.B.E. radio; my father, Deacon Richard C. Vaughn; Neomie McCarthy (I still have that letter you wrote to me when I graduated from college); Pat Kaduk; Jacqueline Penny; Idamer Sidney (and all of those who came out for the book signing at Beacon of Joy Church); Elizabeth Wilson (you are such a sweet and wonderful person for supporting me so much during my book signings at Lincoln University); Yoisha Johnson (for the break-in bookclub event, consistent networking help, and business advice from a phenomenal

MBA graduate); Benecia R. Williams of Lincoln University; Sandra Griffin of Lincoln University (for spreading the word to Alumni Affairs); Touré Muhammad, publisher of "Bean Soup Times"; Terry Livingston; Amazon.com; BarnesandNoble.com; and LuLu.com (for giving me the opportunity to share my craft with a larger audience).

Anytime a book is distributed to the public, it is open for criticism and compliments. I want to thank my loyal readers who took the time to contact me and tell me what worked, what didn't, and spread such kind words: Derek Johnson (my Amazon friend who doesn't pull any punches); Tiliene McGee; Calvin "Phive0Phor" Armstead Jr. (a refreshing and intelligent man whose political/social thoughts are so on point, I give you nothing but respect); Phillip Cavil Sr. of MidWest Family Incorporated (one of my longest and most focused friends since I was 16); Celina Castillo (the BXS8R, thank you for all of the directions and information on New York boroughs); Ain Drew (thank you for your support with PETA, and I wish you the best of luck with your poetry book [If] Life's Rotten, Write to the Core); Jacquette Smith; Charletta Whittenburg; Elvin Carey Jr. (my godfather and the man who refrained from strangling me from all the cursing in Change for a Twenty, love ya); Tiara Sheets; Angel Martin; André Coleman, author of

Blackbirds and *A Liar's Tale*; Cassandra Daniels, author of *Caught in the Middle* and *Together Again*; APOOO Books, Jessica Stafford; Cepheus Edmondson; and Jerome Fitzpatrick (who can dust me in a best handwriting contest any day of the week—you have such a beautiful gift with your artwork and, when time permits, I hope you use that to your economical advantage. I still have the papier mache rose and chalk sign through two moves!).

A big thank you goes out to those who also showed support: Mr. Quirk, my elementary school computer teacher, who always encouraged me to write; my grandfather, my favorite nemesis, and one of the most humble and intelligent people I've ever known, Samuel R. Vaughn (I love you like I love hot water cornbread!); Erin Francis; Jason Chan; Tiffany Tapley of P3 Clothing; Kelli E. Caulfield; Kendra Kemp; Yolanda Coleman (what's up, cuz?); Helen Chang; Jolanta Pomiotlo; Brandon G. Nelson; Tammie Veal; John Albrecht Jr., author of *If Heaven's Forever* ; Karen Siplin, one of my favorite authors of books like *His Insignificant Other* and *Such a Girl*; Mandy Koskiniemi (my unpaid, unlicensed therapist who kept me from losing my mind at Northern Hell-Michigan University); Kari Lindsey; Luke Schierholz (thank you for the phenomenal new covers of *Round Trip*; you are a pleasure to work with, and I'll recommend you wherever I go); Ann M. Martin, author of *The Babysitter's Club* and the first author to ever encourage me to pursue writing; Tom of MySpace.com (for letting promoters use his site free of charge); Trace Brouwn, co-author of *A Writer's Suicide* (I respect your honesty and enjoy your sense of humor—I've just got to convince you to say "bogus," Joe!); Alissia Delaney; Troy Underwood (thank you for the feedback on my Associated Content articles, and no, I'm still not going to eat bacon); Richard-from-across-the-street who would take time from wrestling to check out my short stories; and Ruth O'Brien (for the celebratory lunch at Lao Szechuan and the toast—I was so surprised). To all of the companies like *Fate* magazine, *Citizens in America* magazine, and AssociatedContent.com, who gave me much needed cash for my writing, thank you as well. My bill collectors appreciate AC as well.

I cannot forget my favorite writer and poet ever: Langston Hughes. I have the utmost respect for him. This Harlem Renaissance writer was known for going against the grain and speaking out for what he believed in, from honoring African American women in poems like "Harlem Sweeties" to social issues on "I Too." If you haven't checked him out yet, I'd suggest you start, but wait until you finish this novel please, okay?

Speaking of African American heroes, I want to thank some of the most phenomenal women who I didn't know personally but admired a great deal growing up: Gwendolyn Brooks, Rosa Parks, Maya Angelou, and the baddest sista I've ever read about—Harriet Tubman who freed over 300 slaves and went into enemy territory nineteen times. We have a bunch of people who think they're tough and been through it all, but Mrs. Tubman had to be one of the strongest people I've ever heard of.

Throughout this book, you'll notice I mention music a few times, and that's because I love music with a message. I have a ridiculous CD collection, and I'm still a music video head. I love to see what's new and bump what's legendary. I want to thank positive female hip hop artists like MC Lyte ("Cha Cha Cha" is classic), Queen Latifah, and Salt n' Pepa who showed ladies that you don't have to play yourself to get a man's respect. I also want to thank the folks who are keeping hip hop positive, political, and bold, such as my favorite hip hop emcees Common, Mos Def, Big Daddy Kane ("Smooth Operator" is one of my top ten jams), and James Brown (R.I.P.) for being essential in the making of hip hop and creating songs like "I'm Black and

I'm Proud." I want to thank my favorite R&B artists who I blasted heavily during the creation stages of this book, such as Robin Thicke, Ne-Yo, Usher, the Temptations, and the all-time best R&B artist ever, Marvin Gaye (R.I.P.). Last but absolutely not least, I want to thank some of the most powerful African American men in helping Black folks progress as a culture with unity, strength, and pride: Malcolm X, Frederick Douglass, Martin Luther King Jr., and Johnnie Cochran (R.I.P. to all). I have major respect to the survivors and fighters for Black Wall Street for the injustice done to them in Tulsa, Oklahoma. I often wonder where African American society would be economically should Black Wall Street continued to grow.

All right, now that I'm done thanking the strangers who have no clue who I am, the supporters who don't know me and bought the book anyway and/or promoted it, and the folks I know and love who helped my writing progress, I'll get a move on. Put your seatbelts on and enjoy the round trip.

Part 1

Chapter 1: Cara

"Cara, I don't know how you talked me into this, but if she starts acting up, I'm out," Memo said.

"I promise she won't. Seleste has asked about you a billion times since she told me when her flight lands. What are you worried about? You talked to her all the time while she was in New York," I responded.

"Yeah, but sometimes your girl gets brand new," Memo said.

"It ain't like she could forget about you though. Looking at your ex-girlfriend everyday could have that effect," Jermaine said, looking at Memo and laughing.

Memo shook his head while I continued to look around O'Hare airport. I watched people of various races shuffle by, hugging family members and friends, complaining about overzealous security checking their bags, and listening to the announcement about an orange alert. My best friend, Seleste, had gone to New York for an internship with a legal firm. Under normal circumstances, she would've been happy to go, but the way it went down was almost like she was pushed out of Lace University. She'd gotten into it with another girl at our college, and the administrative faculty put her on academic probation. But, since the internship had already been a done deal, she was allowed to go. Seleste is a little bit of a hothead, but she behaved. Otherwise, she would've been kicked out of school and her transcripts would've been held.

"The belt took forever to roll my luggage around," I heard someone grumble behind me. I turned around to look into the dark brown eyes of the hothead herself.

"Seleste," I squealed and hugged her. We both jerked back and forth, and she squealed as well. "Girl, I'm so glad you could come back in time to get your dress

1

fitted." I looked down at her maroon top, matching the maroon belt and maroon boots she wore, with snug name-brand jeans. "Girl, you are the only vegetarian I know who's thick as cornbread. What did you eat while you were there? Your hips spread." I twirled her around.

"You always do wonders for my self-esteem," she said with a laugh and swatted me on the arm. Before I could hit her back, Jermaine grabbed her into a bear hug. She hugged her childhood friend back just as tight, and swiped her New York Yankees cap from her head in exchange for his White Sox cap. He moved one arm from her waist to take off the cap she'd put on his head.

"Girl, you don't even like sports. What are you doing with this on?" Jermaine said, putting it back on his head.

"I bought it because it was maroon," she said with a grin. Typical Seleste. Always shopping. She turned to me and put her other arm on my shoulder. "Girl, I bought so many clothes that I could dress you and me for the next year."

"I can see that," Memo said. All three of us turned to look at him. I cracked a grin at his cool pose by the lost and found desk. That man was forever acting like he was in front of a camera. Pause. Flash. I looked at Seleste, back to Memo, and took note of the grin spreading across her face. She raised her arms over Jermaine and my shoulders, and wrapped them around Memo, who in turn put his arms around her waist. I beamed from ear to ear when he gave her the too-long hug, when a man uses his fingers to trace a woman's spine. Seleste wasn't shortstopping either because I couldn't get a ruler between those two from the looks of it. I glanced over at Jermaine, who was pretending not to see this little romantic encounter.

"Seleste, how many suitcases do you have?" Jermaine yelled. "No wonder it took you a half hour longer to get to us. These people were probably calling you

Seleste bin Laden," Jermaine said, walking over to two big suitcases and two bags.

She broke her hold on Memo and turned around. "Eh man, I told you I did some damage to the stores." She walked over to Jermaine.

"How did you get all of these over to us?" Jermaine asked, squatting down to put the shoulder strap of one bag over his head.

"I'm swoll," she said, forming her arm into a muscle. Jermaine rolled his eyes and felt her arm. He raised an eyebrow when he tried to jiggle the bottom part of her arm, but it was solid. "See, I told you."

"Whatever, Superwoman. Let's go," he said and grabbed the handle of one of the wheeled suitcases. Memo walked next to Jermaine and pulled the other. She picked up the other bag and pulled it over her shoulder. I took the suitcase that Jermaine was rolling with one arm, and put my other arm around Seleste.

"Somebody is happy to see you," I whispered to her.

She grinned at me and said, "I'm happy to see you too, girl."

I frowned. "Not me, fool."

She laughed and nodded. "I know who you're talking about. I'm just playing."

Although I was talking about Memo, I was glad to have my friend back too. She'd been in New York for all of spring semester and my wedding was on the eighteenth of July, so that left us with only about three months to plan. I wanted to get married before my junior year of college started. It was going to be even more hectic since Jermaine had completed his program and was graduating early in June, with Memo and another of Jermaine's frat members and my ex-fling, Arnez. Jermaine and I were together our senior year of high school, broke up for awhile, and got back together in the spring. Twenty-one years old and I was ready to jump the broom with the love of my life, with his fine, chocolate self. I stared at the back of his athletic frame somewhat hidden underneath his fraternity jacket and tan khakis. Underneath his cap was a Caesar haircut, and a small diamond glimmered from both of his ears. My body shook just thinking about the things I wanted to do to him later. In love is an understatement for what I am with Mr. Ballad. Cara Ballad. Got a nice ring to it, if I do say so myself. He felt my eyes on him and turned around to blow me a kiss. I reached my arm up and wiped it sloppily across my lips in a fake disgusted face.

He chuckled. "See, I'm going to remember you just did that later on," he said. I winked at him.

Seleste looked at both of us and shook her head. "You two are a mess."

I blew Jermaine a kiss and he ducked, looking over his head like it was a gunshot. Memo looked back and laughed at Jermaine's antics. While we went up the escalator to the exit, Seleste and I were a few steps behind, looking in the souvenir shop windows. "Cara, I have to ask you a question."

"Shoot," I said.

"Why are you really going all the way to Atlanta to get married? Why can't we just stay in Chicago and do it? I'm still trying to figure out why you invited Arnez to the wedding."

I shrugged. "Seleste, that's Jermaine's frat brother. I'm not going to disrespect his friends like that, regardless of Arnez and me messing around last year. Plus, Atlanta has more culture. We can have more fun there. They have all the hot HBCUs, the Atlanta History Center, the..."

Seleste rolled her eyes. "Quit playing with me. You don't want to compare scenery, do you? We've got museums here. We go to an HBCU. You know good and well you're not going there to check out schools, and you two are like rabbits, so I know y'all aren't going to leave the room long enough to go see any of the scenery."

"True, true. But, I want to go to grad school in ATL anyway."

"You can go look at schools any time. You still have another year to go before you graduate. Well, if you change your major again, two more years. Or three. Or four."

"Keep playing and I'll make you carry your own damn bag." We stepped off the escalator.

"I just don't get why you'd want to spend all that money on a wedding and then spend the money on traveling too, especially when your family said that they didn't mind coming up here."

"Yeah, but my grandfather is 84. He doesn't need to be traveling that far," I explained. I hadn't seen most of my family during the time I'd been in college because they all lived in Georgia and Louisiana. With Hurricane Katrina, many of my relatives had moved to other places and my wedding would be the first time in a couple years that we'd all be in one spot together. I came to Chicago to live with my older brother, who was married with two sons, but after high school and a semester of college, I decided to live in the dorms to give them some much needed space. I still visited them often with Jermaine in tow.

"Ummm...do you two plan on walking up?" my fiancé yelled over his shoulder.

"Boy, you better relax," Seleste said.

"Y'all are walking all slow like we don't have anywhere to go. Seleste, get up here and talk to Memo. He's getting lonely," Jermaine teased.

She turned to look at me. "I can't stand your man," she said, blushing. I laughed.

"You know you want to be up there by Memo. Don't front," I responded. She made a face at me, but I noticed her speed picked up.

"So are we taking the blue line or what?" she asked us. "Because if we are, we're going the wrong way."

Memo shook his head. "Nah, I have a car now." Seleste's eyes sparkled. I knew what that meant. They were about to talk cars and I was not interested. As much as that chick hated changing oil and anything dealing with auto maintenance, she loved talking about cars and speeding in them even more. Memo and Seleste talked about car makes and models from the exit door until her suitcases were put in the trunk. Jermaine and I got into the back seat of Memo's car, and Seleste scooted into the passenger side.

"Anybody hungry?" Memo asked.

"I'm always hungry," I said. At 120 lbs. and 5'1, I could pretty much eat anything and not gain a pound. Seleste would always lecture me about eating all the fried foods I ate. A burger and fries were my favorite meal and nobody could figure out where the food went. If it wasn't for the D-cups I was sporting, if I walked into a high school right now, I'd fit right in and nobody would question my age.

"Let's go to the Cheesecake Factory," Jermaine said.

"Jermaine, we're supposed to be saving for the wedding."

"I got y'all," Memo said.

I looked at Memo through the rearview mirror. "All right, baller, then have us then. That job with the cops must be paying well."

Seleste whipped her head around. "You're a cop now?"

"Nah, babe. The last thing I want to do is follow in my father's footsteps. I'm still studying law like you though. I've got a clerical job with this parole officer. Busy work. Copying files. Getting donuts. Boring. But hell, it pays the bills."

"Well, I'll pay for my food, but you can treat them," she said.

"You're too proud to take a free meal?" he asked her.

"No, I'm just saying I can pay for myself," she responded.

I shook my head. "Well, both of you can pay for my meal because the down payment on that hall has my money tight." Before Jermaine could open his mouth again, I poked him. I knew he was going to offer to pay for me, but we both needed to pay for the cake, his suit, and the reception food. He sighed and leaned back in the seat. Whenever Jermaine and Seleste got together, I remembered why they'd been friends for so long. Those two had more pride than anybody I knew. I was actually surprised Jermaine and I got back together for that reason alone. He'd gotten a job in California deejaying, it didn't work out, and he came back. I just knew there was no way that he'd try to get back with me after he'd screwed it up by not staying in touch, but low and behold, he was persistent. I guess everybody has a soft spot. I just happened to be his and he was definitely mine.

Chapter 2: Seleste

"I don't care what you say," I said while unpacking my suitcase. "This is just weird how cool you and Arnez are."

Jermaine shrugged. "He was in my ship. I got use to him now. While you were gone, me and him got real cool."

"But don't you think that's going to be weird for Cara? Her ex-boyfriend and her fiancé?"

"She's cool with it though."

"How do you know?"

"Because I asked her, inch high private eye," he said. "You need to be paying more attention to what you're going to do about this sublease."

I sighed. During the time I was in New York, my roommate, C.C., let her boyfriend Jacob take care of my half of the rent, but now that I was back, she still wanted him to stay. I wasn't having it. We found the apartment together so I had as much right to it as she did.

"Jermaine, I don't know what I'm going to do. He's over here so much that I'm wondering if he shouldn't be paying rent again. When I came home yesterday, that fool was walking around butt naked."

Jermaine laughed. "Your first time seeing one of them things, huh?"

I squinted my eyes at him. "Eh, I may not have walked through the gate, but trust me, I've seen the map to get there."

We both laughed and he gave me dap. "I see your directions led you back to Memo though. The way Cara told it, you two have been talking the whole time you were on the east coast."

"Cara can't keep anything to herself, huh?" I walked to my closet to hang up a few shirts. "Yeah, Cara gave him my number. He felt bad about the whole fight with Lisa."

"I know he had to love how you fought for him though," he said, taking a pair of socks from my suitcase. He laid back on my bed, tossing them up and catching them.

I caught the socks on the way down. "How many times do I have to tell you that I did not fight for Memo? I fought because she was starting mess."

He turned around and grabbed another pair of socks. "Yeah, all right, Seleste. Whatever you say."

I smacked my lips. "So did Cara already let her family know she needed a church out there?"

Jermaine yawned. "Yeah, her grandfather is taking care of that. It's going to be at his church. But back to your original question, Arnez isn't going to do anything. Me and that dude talked about it. He wished us both the best of luck. He's like my brother and that kind of bond isn't breakable. I can't see him acting stupid at our wedding anyway."

I shook my head. "I can. I personally think you two shouldn't invite him, but you're going to do what you want to anyway." I walked over to my computer chair and sat down. "What would you do if he stood up during the part of the speech when the preacher talks about anybody being against the wedding?"

"He's already going to be standing. He's a groomsman."

"Jermaine, you know what I mean."

He stopped throwing my socks and faced me. "What do you want me to say? Whoop his ass?"

I leaned back against the desk. "I would."

Jermaine scratched his forehead. "Seleste, you can't fight your way out of everything. I'd see what Cara did first."

9

"I don't think she'd be so calm. She'd probably flip out on him for doing that."

"Then that's that." He laid back on the bed and closed his eyes. I knew my best friend well. When he closed his eyes, he was thinking. Jermaine and I grew up around each other. He was friends with one of my neighbors and that branched off into us being friends. I went to elementary school with Cara, but she and I spent more time hanging out at lunch rather than around our homes. Cara went to Atlanta to stay with her grandparents each summer and bounced around with various relatives during the school year. Even when Cara's grandmother passed away, she still went back every summer to hang with her grandfather. Jermaine and I got closer because we went to the same southside high school, while Cara went to a high school on the northside of Chicago. The two of them met for the first time at my seventeenth birthday party, and as soon as I saw them interact, I knew they'd end up together. Arnez was also from Atlanta and moved to Chicago, and Cara spent a lot of time in Atlanta but lived here as well, and they both found that connection during the time that Jermaine and Cara briefly split up. But as expected, Cara and Jermaine found their way back to each other.

Jermaine could act like the possibility of Arnez playing the jealous role was out of the ordinary, but we all had been exposed to enough of Arnez's drama to know that he would do something like that. I wasn't convinced that Arnez had changed all that much in the semester I'd been gone. With the sexual relationship he'd had with Cara, the crush he'd had on me, and him hopping to other women, he was one of those dudes who loved being promiscuous but didn't understand how any woman could possibly cheat on him. Absolutely vain. Vain mixed with some respect on campus and with the ladies made him even more difficult to deal with.

*　　　*　　　*

"So how long are you going to keep this a secret?" Memo asked me. I swung my legs on his lap and leaned on the bench. Looking out at the blue water of Lake Michigan always put me at ease. I looked around at other couples laying on the grass, sitting in their parked cars, or fishing. Irving Park's boat area was one of the places I missed most about Chicago while I was gone. I twirled the kitchen area of my hair with my arm resting on the back of the bench. Looking at Memo, I puckered my lips and he reciprocated, leaning towards me for a kiss.

"You didn't answer my question," he whispered in my ear and kissed my neck. I shrugged. He pulled me closer so I was on his lap. "I missed you." I laughed when he said that. Memo was such a cake, and I loved every minute of it.

"You should have."

Before I could blink, I'd landed on the grass. I scooted on my elbows and laughed. "You're abusive." He didn't laugh. Muffing his head, I sat down next to him again. Before I could open my mouth again to respond, a car rolled by behind us blasting a popular hip hop song. We both bobbed our heads to it and recited the lyrics. Hip hop was like that. The whole world could be doing you wrong, but when your jam was on, all was okay. When the car's music softened as the driver moved on, Memo's face hardened again.

"So, you're going to pout now?" I asked him.

"Seleste, do you ever get tired of acting like a child?"

I raised an eyebrow and cocked my head to the side. "Excuse me."

He moved a couple inches away from me. Somehow the eighty degree weather cooled off when he

11

distanced himself. "You make me feel like I'm the female in this relationship. Why are you so hard to get through to?"

I sighed. I'd heard this comment a thousand times from different guys. I was well-known for being the woman who refused to put her heart into a relationship. Call it foolish pride. I liked to call it a safety net though, but I knew sooner or later, the guard would have to come down a little. When Memo asked to take the relationship a step further during my time in NY, I agreed. He made it plain that he was in it all or nothing and before I accepted being his girlfriend, I had to know that. I liked his confidence, so I agreed. "All right, when do you want me to tell them we're together?" I asked Memo.

"Man, you do what you feel."

I sighed. "I just said I'd tell them, and you're still mad."

He stood up. I watched his muscular frame and noticed his Scorpion tattoo was different. He'd added the symbol that looked like the letter *m* and *emo* was diagonally drawn through the scorpion's tail. I followed the veins in his athletic arms up to the back of his neck. Memo's curly hair was tapered low around the sides and he had small sideburns. Damn it, this dude looked good. He turned around to see me grinning.

"What are you grinning about?" he snapped.

"Remember Ne-Yo's song about liking women when they're mad?" I asked.

He shook his head. "I can't believe you're trying to game me." I laughed and started singing the words to the song. "I need to stop messing with you." I knew he didn't mean it because his mouth was fighting a smile. I started singing louder and off key. I ended the song by dialing Cara's phone number with my cell phone. He looked at the water while the phone rang. It went to voicemail.

"Hey yo, I'm out and about doing my thing. Leave a message for Cara."

"Hey Cara, just wanted to let you know what me and my...boyfriend," I started. Memo whipped his head around and noticed the phone in my hand. "We just wanted to say hello." I clicked the switch button when I heard a beeping noise letting me know there was an incoming call. It was Cara. "Hey girl."

"What's up? You called," she said.

I looked up at Memo staring at me and bit my lip.

"Hello?" Cara said.

"Yeah."

"Seleste, what'd you call me for?"

"Check your voicemail."

"Why can't you tell me what the message is?"

"Just check it."

"Oh gawd, fine then." She disconnected the call.

Memo and I watched a sailboat float by. "I still can't figure out how those boat people don't fall in the water leaning on them like that," I said. He didn't respond. I guess small talk was out of the question. My phone rang again.

"Who's your boyfriend?" Cara cooed.

I laughed. "Who do you think?"

"Aww. For how long?"

I counted days with my fingers. "About a month and a half. You already know how much he and I talked while I was in New York."

"Took you long enough to admit it. I already knew though. Jermaine does too."

"How'd you two know?"

"Girl please. You two at the airport was too obvious. Did you really think we didn't figure it out? You didn't know about his car or his job, for real?"

I blushed through the phone. "Nah, I knew. Just playing the role."

"Badly."

"Whatever," I said. Memo looked at me again and sat down. "I got to go."

"Why?" she asked.

"He's sitting next to me," I said. She cooed again, and I groaned. "This has got to be the lamest conversation ever. Goodbye, Cara." She laughed and I clicked the end button and looked at Memo. "So I told her. Who else do you want me to tell besides Cherese?"

His eyes widened at the sound of his ex-girlfriend's name. I'd worked with her regularly during the internship in New York. "Who said anything about Cherese?"

"I already told her while I was there."

"Why?"

My lip curled into a snarl. "I wanted her to stop calling you."

He nodded. "She didn't." Now it was my turn to be pissed.

Chapter 3: Memo

I've dealt with all types of women. Thick ones. Thin ones. Short ones. Tall ones. Long hair. Short hair. Brown skinned. Light skinned. But one thing they all had in common was they were crazy as hell. I can't find a sane woman to save my life, but eh, it ain't like I'm wrapped too tight either. I was about to graduate and didn't need the stress of a relationship, but Seleste was cool. I dug her most of the time, and all that attitude she tried to have went right out the window when we would eventually do the damn thing. Yeah, I said eventually. No sex. Not yet. But with a little time, I knew I'd break her in. I've dealt with virgins before. A month tops and I was in there. Seleste was away for an internship for a semester so I guessed that now she was back in Chicago, I was on day nine. I had twenty-one more days to go.

I met her through Cara, this lady that use to mess with my friend Arnez. Problem was that the same time I was trying to see where Seleste's head was, my ex-girlfriend, Cherese, was still in the picture. Funny how things work out. I left New York to get away from my father's legal situation and Cherese's scandalous ways, and both of them motherfuckers followed me to Chicago. My father got out of jail after serving some time for selling drugs, as a cop, and Cherese came here to try to get me back.

My parents were separated but my mother took my father, Terrell, back. I, however, didn't get back with Cherese. I was tired of her. She kept up too much drama, she was a golddigger, and way too sarcastic. But my brother, Jeremiah, loved her. Even when she went back to Brooklyn, she still called me and Jeremiah still called her. Strange thing was that Seleste ended up in New York too. Seleste never really said too much about working with her, but she and I kept in touch. I dodged asking her about Cherese because I didn't want her to think I still loved my ex, plus they'd met once when Cherese came to Chicago and the encounter wasn't friendly at all. Seleste dodged asking me about Cherese because she didn't want to look jealous. Cherese, on the other hand, fed off of that. I think her favorite hobby for those three months was messing with Seleste's head.

"Here comes your little girlfriend," she called me and said one time.

I rolled my eyes and cursed myself for not checking the caller i.d. before I picked up the phone.

"Cherese, I don't know how many times I got to tell you to stop calling me," I said.

"Memo, do you still love me?"

I paused. "Why do you ask me that every single time you talk to me?"

"I just don't get how you could still love someone and not want to be with them."

"Cherese, I love the smell of collard greens, but that doesn't mean I want to eat them everyday."

"Remember when you use to eat..."

"Okay! That's enough of that conversation. Stop calling me."

"Wait Memo. Look, are you and Seleste really together? That's what she told me."

"And what do you believe?"

"I believe that she's too far away to really be with you."

"Hate to break it to you, ma, but you're in the same state she is, so how are you different?"

"We have five years together and history before then."

"And now all we have is history."

Cherese paused. I knew that would annoy her. After a few seconds, I heard a click. She'd hung up. I still hadn't confirmed whether Seleste and I were together. I felt like a hypocrite. Besides Cherese's golddigging ways, distance was also an issue with us. But the difference was that Seleste was coming back after one semester. Cherese represented for Brooklyn more than Caesar from the Boondocks comic strip so I knew she wasn't going anywhere. There was another issue too. Lisa, the lady Seleste got into the fight with, was expelled because of that. I was trying to be good to Seleste, but a brotha was about to bust if she didn't give it up soon. I was ready to rape myself.

*   *   *

"Memo, would you stop playing?" Seleste said. I kept on kissing her neck. Her hair smelled like shampoo and her neck smelled like perfume.

"C'mon Seleste. Get off the computer," I whispered in her ear. I massaged her breasts underneath her shirt. After a few seconds, she stood up and leaned into me, walking backwards to my bed. She laid on top of me and started pulling up my shirt.

"Hey Memo, phone for you," my younger brother, Jeremiah, yelled.

Seleste kept kissing me. I cupped her ample hips and listened to her moan softly. Jeremiah knocked on my door.

I frowned. "I heard you," I snapped at him. I heard the knob twirl, but my door was locked. As soon as Seleste left, I was going to crack that boy upside the head for trying to open a grown man's door. Seleste scooted off of me and laid down on my pillows. Jeremiah knocked again.

I jumped up from my bed and snatched it open. "What?"

Jeremiah growled back. "I said you had a phone call." That fool had the audacity to strut away like it was

17

nothing. I was definitely going to light his ass up when Seleste left. I stormed into the living room and snatched up the phone.

"What?" I yelled.

I heard sniffling.

"Hello," I said a little softer.

"Memo," my mother said. "Your father snapped."

I leaned the phone against my shoulder, adjusted my high school graduation ring, and reached for my boots sitting next to the nearby couch. "What'd you just say?"

"I can't believe it. We're married but he had no right to put his hands on me and…"

"To what?" I interrupted her.

Pause. I repeated myself.

"Forget it. I shouldn't have called you," my mother said.

I gritted my teeth. "Ma, is Terrell still there?" Ever since my father had been locked up for selling drugs as an undercover cop, I'd had trouble calling him Dad. Before his sentencing, it was second nature. Now, it felt forced. My mother didn't answer. I hung up the phone and grabbed my car keys from the coffee table.

"What's wrong?" I heard Seleste say. I turned around to see her standing by the door with her coat on and cell phone in hand. She must've seen me getting ready to go. I stared at her. She opened the door and we both walked to my car.

"Memo, can I come?" Jeremiah yelled out the door. At thirteen years old, I didn't really want him to deal with this kind of drama. But I needed him to understand that it was never okay to hit a woman, especially not our mother. Seleste was already sitting in the passenger seat talking on her phone. I looked from her to Jeremiah and wondered whether I should go alone. But if I went alone, I might end up behind bars like my ex-con father was for the past few years. I turned to look at Jeremiah again. "Nah, Jay, stay here," I said, calling him by his nickname. He frowned and slammed the door.

He'd been acting a fool for the past few months that he'd stayed in my apartment. I couldn't tell whether it was because he was mad about my mother wanting to have space to be with my father or just being a teenager. I'd deal with him later. I ran around to the driver's side and got in the car. Seleste closed her flip phone, I burned rubber out of the parking spot, and she calmly put on her safety belt. She reached around me and pulled at mine. I tried to wiggle away, but she grabbed my hand and fastened it. We pulled up to my parents' house a few minutes later, and I ran to the door with my keys out. Seleste was on the phone again and hadn't come up to the porch. I unlocked my parents' door and walked in.

"Mom!" I yelled. I looked around and saw all the furniture in place. I yelled for her again and climbed the stairs. I heard footsteps behind me and turned around to see my mother coming from the kitchen. I jumped down the steps two at a time and grabbed her. I looked for marks and saw none, but she was crying. My mother was a small woman, about 5'3 and at the most, 135 lbs. With such a small frame, she was notorious for wearing fitted clothes, but that day she wore a Rosa Parks oversized t-shirt and khaki capris. I looked down at her capris and noticed a couple of burgundy spots. I looked back up at her face. She moved away from me, but I yanked her back by her shirt. My breath shortened when I caught a glimpse of a whip on her back. I grabbed the railing and almost fell to my knees.

"Where is he?" I asked.

"He left," she said quietly.

"What happened?"

"He tried to…Memo, I don't know how to tell you this."

"Just say it."

19

She bit her lip. My mother was never the nervous type. She always looked sharp. Hair always neatly flat-ironed. Corporate casual wear. The same hazel eyes as Jeremiah. But now she just looked tired. "I think I may have HIV."

I looked up at her, not believing what she'd said. "For how long?"

"The disease or when did I get it?"

"When did you get it?"

"I don't know if I have it. I don't even know if you can get it every time."

"What are you talking about? Did he cheat on you?"

She shook her head. "He was raped in jail. I never told you, but I knew. Neither of us knew he had the disease though."

"So, what does that have to do with you having HIV?"

She shrugged. "I refused to have sex with him until he got tested."

I frowned. "So he has HIV?"

"His counselor said he does. I didn't...I didn't let him have sex with me. He tried to force me to."

My nose flared. "He raped his own wife?"

She started crying. Out of the corner of my eye, I saw Seleste walk in the hallway with Jermaine nearby. My mother looked up. "Who's he?" she asked me. I looked down blankly at the floor.

"This is my best friend, Jermaine," Seleste said to my mother, but I could feel her looking at me. "I called him. I didn't know if Memo needed help."

Jermaine walked over to me and leaned over. "What's going on? Seleste told me you looked like you were about to whoop somebody's..." He stopped before he cursed and lowered his voice. "Do we need to handle something?"

I walked past him and to the front door. I needed some air. When I stepped outside, I saw our mutual friend, O, sitting on the porch.

"What's up, bruh?" O greeted me wearily. I sat down on the porch and put my head in my hands. As soon as Seleste wrapped her arms around me, my tears spilled into her hair.

Chapter 4: Jermaine

Seleste called me talking about Memo storming out the door like it was about to be some problems. That's my boy, so I had to make sure he was all right, especially when Seleste was too hardheaded to stay at his house instead of following him.

"Seleste, where is he at?" I said into the phone.

"He's talking to his brother."

"Where is he going?"

"I heard him say something to his mother. This is crazy. I hope it's nothing bad. I don't want to meet her for the first time if it's some drama going on."

"Yeah well, I'm on my way. Hit me back when you get there."

"'Kay," she said and hung up the phone. O and I were chilling at Harold's restaurant. I explained to my boy what was going on on the way there. The friendship between him, me, Jermaine, and our friend, Arnez, was a little complex. O and Arnez were friends before college, and they met Memo while all of them were on the football team. Arnez didn't like me too much because he thought Cara still liked me. Obviously she did, but I have to admit that I had a lot to do with that because I was determined to get her back. Arnez wasn't treating her right, which made the situation even easier to just slide right in. Arnez and I ended up being cool because we both pledged into the best fraternity on campus. When you go through something like that, then previous animosity seems tedious. Memo and O figured if he and I were so cool, they'd reach out too. Now the four of us are tighter than a spandex dress.

"So how do you know we're going to the right place?"

"I don't. But she said she would..."

My cell phone rang. "Yeah," I answered.

"He just went in the house," Seleste said.

"We're about ten minutes away," I replied.

"All right," she said.

"Gone," I said and hung up.

O turned on my cd player and started flexing.

"What are you doing?" I asked.

"Eh, we got to listen to fight music on the way. Get us charged," he said, throwing imaginary punches.

I laughed. O was definitely the comedian of the group. He was also the oldest of the crew. Who knows when he'll graduate. He changes his major more than my fiancée. I turned onto Cicero and sped past the mall and the retail stores. We both jumped out the car as soon as I pulled up.

"Hey, I'll stay outside in case something goes wrong," O said.

I nodded and reached up to ring the doorbell, but saw the door wide open. I knew it had to be something serious if folks were leaving their doors open on the southside of Chicago. I looked through the screen door and saw his mother facing the stairs. She was sitting on the floor. I opened the door and saw Seleste in the living room on my right-hand side. I whistled low and she looked over. She put her finger to her mouth and then her ear. We both listened to the conversation and were beyond words. Finally, we walked closer to them and I went to Memo. Before I got more than a few words out, he stood up and I followed. I couldn't imagine how I'd take some news like that so I couldn't blame my boy for crying. I watched Seleste comfort him and O looked shocked as he sat on one of the steps. I motioned for O to walk with me to my car and explained the situation.

"So what do you want to do now?" O asked me.

I shrugged. "It's up to Memo and his mother. If they call the police, that fool is going to jail for good."

"And if they don't?"

"Eh, I'm for whatever Memo wants to do." I walked back to the porch and sat down on one of the stoops. O sat on the one across from me. My cell rang and I looked at the caller i.d. Speak of the devil.

"Waddup," I said.

"What's going on with you, Beatz?" Arnez said in an exaggerated southern drawl.

"Some of everything. Let me call you back."

"You sound mad. What's the deal?"

"Nah, I'm good."

"Where you at then?"

"Memo's mom's house. But let me hit you back."

"All right then." I pressed the end button. Memo stopped crying while Seleste rubbed his back.

"I know this sounds like a dumb question, but Memo, what do you want us to do?" O asked.

Memo's jaw tightened. "Leave so there are no witnesses."

I stood up. "Whoa. I can't do all that. I know you're mad right now but both of y'all in jail ain't gonna change the situation."

Memo stood up. "Naw, fuck that. That man basically is trying to kill my mother." Spit flew from his mouth as he waved his arms wildly.

I looked across the street at an older woman peeking out of her window. "Memo, dawg, lower your voice a little. Everybody on the block doesn't need to know the situation."

"I couldn't give a fuck who knows. I'm going to kill that dude when I see him." He jumped down the stairs and started pacing back and forth. I looked at O for help but he was clenching his jaw too. As much as he joked around, when O was serious, you knew the situation was heavy. I looked up at Seleste to see if she'd talk some sense into him, but my friend is not exactly the most level-headed woman you'd ever meet. Since we were little, she always operated off of emotions first, practicality later. Memo paced back and forth a few more times and suddenly climbed all eight of the bungalow steps in two leaps. I thought he was going to see if his mother was okay, but then I heard her yelling at him.

"Memo! Stop!" she shrieked.

O and I hopped around Seleste on the steps and into the house. Renee, Memo's mother, was wrestling with him in the living room.

"Stop it. I don't want you to end up in jail," she said, leaping on his back.

"Mom, get off of me," he said, trying to pull her legs from around his waist.

For a small woman, she sure had a lot of strength because she managed to make him fall on the couch. I didn't know what to do. If I pulled his mother off, Memo might do something he'd regret later. If she didn't let Memo go, then how was the situation going to be resolved? There was no way O and I were going to let Terrell back in the house, especially not to face Memo. Memo was two inches shorter than his 6'1 father and about forty pounds lighter, thanks to Terrell's jailhouse weight lifting, but I'd seen Memo perform in football. Dude was no punk.

Memo pulled away from his mother and sat down next to her, with his mother's hands wrapped tightly around his arms. Seleste sat next to them.

"Mrs. Martin, my name is Seleste," she said. Renee turned to look at Seleste and then noticed the others in the room. For the first time, I think it really sunk in to her that we were all here and regardless of how personal this topic was, we all knew it so there was no way she could back out now. "What would you like us to do?"

"I don't know," she answered.

"Look at your legs," Memo said sadly. I glanced down to see the bruises on her legs. While struggling with

Memo, her capri shorts had risen slightly. I looked a little closer and realized that the spots were blood.

"Mrs. Martin, we need to get you to a hospital," I said.

She looked down. "No, I'll be all right."

I shook my head. "No, those bruises weren't like that when I first came in the door. You're bleeding now. We need to get you to a hospital." She shook her head. I guess it was time to wrestle his mother again. Memo twisted her arms and picked her up like a rag doll. For some strange reason, she didn't fight him back until we got to the door. Then she jumped out of his arms.

"Put me down. I don't want the neighbors to see me like this. I have to change clothes," she said.

O shook his head. "Nah, if you go in just like that, the hospital will take care of you quicker."

She bit her lip and pondered that before turning around to open the door.

"I'll ride with you two," Seleste said to me and O. "I think Memo and his mother need to talk in the car." O and I nodded. We followed Memo and Renee out to Memo's car and then I went to my own. I knew when we got to the hospital, the doctors would want to call the police. And if Terrell went to jail this time for rape, he'd probably be in there for a long time. Then again, drug dealers stayed in jail longer than rapists, so maybe not.

*   *   *

"This is so messed up," Seleste mumbled from the backseat of my car. She leaned her head against the window.

"Yeah it is," was all I could think to say.

"I feel like I should be there," she said.

"This is family business though, Seleste," O said. I leaned my elbow on the armrest and followed Memo's car.

A few minutes later, Memo parked in front of the emergency room, and he and Renee rushed into the building before I parked. As soon as the car was stationary, Seleste took off running after them, but me and O lagged behind.

"This is wild," O said.

I nodded my head and leaned against my car. "I wouldn't even know what to do now. Should we go find him?"

O rolled his eyes. "Two young brothers like us stomping an ex-cop? Why don't we just kill ourselves now and save the rest of 5-0 the trouble?"

"Doubt that. Dude went to jail. They might not be helping him like that anymore."

"Jermaine, if I went to jail right now, would you stop having my back?"

I nodded. "Good point." My eyes lit up. "But Mr. Martin has to find somewhere to lay low. I don't think he's stupid enough to go to Memo's crib though."

"He was stupid enough to try to rape his own wife."

We both looked at each other and without another word, jumped back in the car.

Chapter 5: Cara

I frowned as I kneeled on my couch and watched cars go by. Jermaine was supposed to drop me off before I went to Atlanta to see my family and check out wedding locations. I'd called his phone, but it kept going to voicemail so I gave up and jumped on the blue line. I called my grandfather to make sure he was still picking me up by our usual meeting spot: a huge colorful statue of a suitcase with a bunch of license plates on it. I'd been to my Atlanta home sporadically throughout the years, bouncing from Chicago for school and Atlanta over the summer until I lived with my brother for most of high school and college. My father was nonexistent and my mother was trying to rekindle her teenage years for all of my adolescence so I was pretty much raised by my maternal grandparents. My late grandmother was one of those Southern women who could outcook anybody's hot water cornbread and collard greens. She worked in a factory by day and still made it home to cook for Grandad before he got home from the same factory. How two people could be married for forty-nine years and work in the same place amazed me. I think I'd have to strangle Jermaine if he and I worked together. My fiancé was completely engulfed in music and wanted to be a deejay and radio host anyway. Although I liked to dance to music, I still didn't know what I wanted to be. In the mean time, I braided hair professionally.

I'd changed my major a billion times but I made sure to get the universal credits out of the way. One of my electives lead me wondering if I should take cosmetology classes, but Seleste and Jermaine talked me out of it.

After I'd checked in my luggage, gotten my boarding pass, and adjusted myself by the window seat of the plane, I was ready to get to work reading some bridal magazines.

*   *   *

I wanted to marry Jermaine since the first time I saw him at Seleste's birthday party back in high school. I thought he was the reason the Earth turned and fell harder for him than anybody else. In every relationship, it always seemed like I liked the guys more than the guys liked me, so I'd become use to it. Regardless of him pursuing me while I was messing around with Arnez, I use to wonder whether Jermaine felt the same way about me until Christmas break. Jermaine and I had gone downtown to shop on the Magnificent Mile and when we headed to Bennigan's for dinner, he asked me to walk over to the Buckingham Fountain with him. I looked at him oddly. The water wouldn't be on and the pretty colors wouldn't be lit up, but I went anyway.

Surprisingly, it wasn't even that cold that day. It was about forty-five degrees, and for Chicago, that's damn near fall weather. We stood by the gate and I was looking at the four sea horses surrounding the fountain when Jermaine handed me the shirt in one of my bags that I'd bought for my brother.

"What are you doing? Put it back in the bag."

He shook his head. "The ground is too cold to be kneeling without a bag." I was confused by why he was flapping a shopping bag around on the ground and kneeled on it, and I noticed a few joggers slowed down on Congress Parkway. I peered down at him.

"Did you lose something?" I asked and tried to kneel down too.

He laughed and pushed me back to standing position. Then I figured out what he was about to do and yelled "Yes!"

He smacked his forehead. "Cara, you have to let me ask you first."

I rocked from side to side and said, "Doesn't matter. My answer is yes."

He laughed and cleared his throat, but before he could open his mouth again, I waved my left hand in front of him. He shook his head, still laughing, and pulled a small jewelry box from his left pocket. He opened it slowly and my mouth became desert dry when I saw a pair of hoop earrings inside.

"Are you kidding me?" I mumbled.

He stared at me seriously and winked. "Yup."

He reached into his right pocket and pulled out another jewelry box. He opened it slowly, and I saw the two karat diamond ring inside. My heart dropped.

"I put this in my right pocket because you're right. Right about me wanting to marry you. You are the right one for me. You are my right-hand woman. But right about now, I need your left hand." He grinned and I held it out. "So does that mean you'll marry me?"

I nodded excitedly like I hadn't already given him an answer, and he stood up and kissed me. I heard clapping over my shoulder and saw that some of the joggers had come closer.

*   *   *

"I wish somebody could make me smile like that," I heard a woman's voice say. I looked up to see the stewardess smiling at me. I waved the fingers on my left hand, and she gasped.

"What a pretty ring," she said. That's all it took for me to launch off into a conversation about how Jermaine proposed.

"Wow. You look so young," she said.

"I'm 21."

Slowly I watched her smile turn into concern. "You said you two have been together for a few months?"

30

"No. Longer than that. We were off and on since high school."

"Marriage is a big step."

My forehead creased into a frown. "Don't you think I know that?"

Suddenly she must've realized she'd struck a nerve because she turned to hold up an apple juice and an orange juice container. "I'm sorry. Maybe I've crossed the line. Would you like something to drink, sweetheart?"

My face tightened. At that moment, I finally understood why Seleste thought pet names were so condescending. Instead of answering her, I turned to look out of the window. I heard her cart moving on, and she greeted the passengers behind me.

"Excuse me," I heard someone say.

I turned to look at the guy sitting across from me. The seat next to me was empty, so I leaned over. "Yes?"

The fair-skinned man with brown freckles scattered on his face pointed behind him. He looked like he was in his late fifties with his neat, pewter suit and matching hat. "Don't pay attention to anything she says. My wife and I got married when we were in our early twenties. We were your age actually, and we've been married for thirty-four years."

I unlatched my seatbelt and moved over to the empty plane seat closer to him. "How did you two stay together so long?"

He took off his hat and sat it on his lap. "We stopped listening to what everybody else had to say about our relationship."

I nodded. "Did anybody think you were too young to get married?"

"Only people in your generation would say something like that. When I was your age, it was standard to get married around that time."

31

"Why do you think more women my age don't get married now?"

"Honey please. It's not like eligible bachelors are standing in line," another voice said. I looked behind the older gentleman to see a woman who looked to be in her thirties staring at me. I looked her over from the light blonde weave with her black roots showing to the extremely snug purple spandex top and black faded jeans. I wondered if she realized her appearance might've been half the problem. I looked at my own outfit, boot-cut capris, an apricot top that fit snugly around my chest and loose around the stomach, and matching heels. My hair was cut short on top with stacks and feathered out around the sides. I always thought I was pretty attractive but had my fair share of lonely nights so I knew looks didn't always matter.

I turned back to her. "What's your idea of eligibility?"

The man across from me turned around to see the lady.

"Girl, I've had 'em all and seen 'em all. Four kids by four different assholes and I've decided men ain't shit."

Suddenly I heard the wheels of the food cart. "Excuse me, ma'am, but I'm going to have to ask you to refrain from using that type of language," the know-it-all stewardess I'd spoken with earlier said.

"I'm just telling it like it is, Miss Lady," the lady said.

"I understand. Would you mind keeping your voice down?" the stewardess asked.

"Who's going to make me?" she said, cocking her head to the side.

I looked at the stewardess, who leaned over to talk to the angry, female passenger, but not before I had to catch myself from laughing at the Cheshire cat grin on Mr. Married's eyes as he checked out her bottom. I couldn't hear what was being said, but when the stewardess stood up again, Ms. Eligible was quiet. The stewardess smiled at me and continued her stroll to the front.

"What happened?" he mouthed to me. I shrugged. He twirled his finger by his ear and pointed behind him. I smiled politely, looked back at Ms. Eligible struggling not to open her mouth again, and I switched back to my window seat. Immediately afterwards, the announcement came on to buckle our seatbelts for landing. I looked over again at Mr. Married, who was now looking out of his right window. He'd said Ms. Eligible was crazy, but I was starting to wonder if I was. Maybe I was too young to get married after all.

*   *   *

"How was the plane ride, Punkin?" my grandfather asked me when I greeted him by the suitcase statue.

"Very strange," I said, wrapping my arms around him. "I'll tell you later though. Let's go get my bags." We walked back inside. We'd always met at that suitcase statue because it was easier to spot each other than by the luggage area. "How are you?"

He shrugged. "Every time I take a shower, I get another dot on my back and arms." He pointed to his arm filled with liver spots. "I'm convinced that when they connect, I'm going to die."

I laughed. "You're so morbid, Grandad."

He reached for one of my bags. "Don't get old, sugar. It's not fun." I reached for the bag he was holding, but he snatched it back. "I'm not too old to hold a bag." I held my hands up and looked for the next one.

"Yes, sir," I said, hiding a smile. My grandfather was a very proud man, and I knew when to pick my arguments. This wasn't one of those times.

"So where's the boy?" he asked.

33

"The man," I corrected.

"Young'un, please. I'm 84 years old. You don't really expect me to think he's grown, do you?"

"I bet you thought you were grown at 21."

"I wish I was 21 right now."

I looked over the belt and saw my other bag nearby. I reached for it and then we both strolled off to his car. "Can I drive?" I asked him.

He squinted his eyes at me. "Why do you always want to drive when you're with me?"

I shrugged. "I like to drive."

"Well, I'm all about doing what my granddaughter likes to do," he said, kissing me on the forehead. I smiled up at him. My grandfather was a cute man. Complexion of tea with a little lemon juice, eyes the color of toast, medium height, and slim build. He wore a matching hat and shoes no matter where he went. I'd seen him in gym shoes enough times to count and all of his dress shoes looked like he'd polished them the same day.

"You look like a seasoned model," I said, checking out his gray dress shirt, gray dress pants, and black shoes. I reached up to touch his hat and he leaned back.

"Seasoned? I'm old. But you touch my hat again and we're going to fight up in here."

I laughed and balled up my fists. I stood in fighting stance.

"Girl, you ain't brave," he said, moving me out of the way as we neared the car. He opened the driver's side door to let me in.

"Chivalry is not dead," I said, sitting down.

"Not as long as your Grandad is here," he said, tapping the car roof and walking around to the passenger side of the car. It felt good to be home. I knew with him around, planning for this wedding would be a breeze.

Chapter 6: Memo

There was a message on my answering machine from O saying that Jeremiah had been dropped off at Arnez's dorm. Jeremiah had hung out with my boy, Arnez, several times since I met him during my junior year of college. I knew he was straight there overnight. Seleste followed me into my apartment and to my bedroom. She sat next to me as I laid on my bed and started running her fingers through my hair. The head massage relaxed my shoulders and I sighed. I had no idea what to do about Terrell. On one hand, if I beat him down, he'd obviously fight back and both of us would end up in jail. He may go in for the other year he was originally supposed to serve, but they let him out early after four with much negotiation. I could care less about him going back, but my issue was that I might go too. I spent a weekend in jail for getting caught, by a cop, with drugs on me. I was trying to get money to bail my father out of jail and my 9-to-5 wouldn't have gotten me the money quick enough. The cops did my father a favor by freeing me, but he still went. I was warned not to get into trouble again, and my mother forced my brother and me to move from New York to Chicago with her while she arranged for a divorce. Love is a funny thing though because when he got out of jail, she ran right back to him. I still don't understand the logic in us moving to have the same life we had in New York.

"I wish I could've been there. I should've never moved out," I mumbled. Seleste moved closer to me and laid her body next to mine. She lifted my shirt slightly and stroked the hair above my belly button. That was all it took. The one thing that could take my mind off of this nightmare was getting some. I looked at her to see if she could tell what I was thinking, and to my surprise, her eyes said she had the same thing on her mind as well. I moved her body on top of mine, but she quickly squirmed under me. Not a problem. I liked being in control. I was never that cat hopping on every piece I saw, but I knew my way around a woman.

I put my hands between her legs and touched that warm area between them. It suddenly struck me that I'd never gotten this far before. When Seleste left for the internship, the furthest I'd gotten was kissing her. But I didn't know what she'd done while she was in New York, regardless of talking to her almost every single day. Maybe she'd been with somebody before me. It seemed a little convenient that she used this moment to let me get at her. Whatever. I'd take it however she gave it to me. No time for questions.

I lifted her shirt and flicked my tongue over her nipples. Her legs immediately roped my waist. Hot zone. I scooted up to kiss her and slyly reached between my mattress and its stand to pull out a condom within a hidden bag. I always kept them close because you never wanted to give a woman the opportunity to change her mind.

"Wait," she whispered.

Fuck. I spoke too soon. I dropped my head on her shoulder and nibbled on her neck.

"Memo," she breathed.

I cupped her butt and laid myself right in that spot I wanted to get more acquainted with.

"Travis," she said.

Aw man, she just called me by my real name. I kissed her lips long and hard. She wrapped her arms around my neck and I moved the bottom half of me up to unzip my khakis. They were already baggy so it didn't take much for them to slide down. I pulled my boxer briefs down while I kept kissing her. Once I was free from the waist down, I brainstormed on how I was going to get her out of her clothes without my government name coming up again. I went right back to her chest and while she moaned, I unbuttoned her shirt and unhooked her bra. Before she knew it, my girl was braless, pantiless, and the only thing on her was her skirt wrapped around her waist. I looked down at her candy brown skin and knew I was going to demolish this woman. I lifted her legs up a little and put my head right in the dark brown hair not on her head.

She clamped her legs closed, and I pulled them open again. I looked up at her wondering if it was her first time for this too. Judging from her nervous expression, I knew it was. "Seleste, let me handle this." I guess my eyes looked confident enough because within a couple minutes, she was pressing my head into her lower region. That's what I was talking about. When she sounded like she was about to hyperventilate, I moved north and kissed around her belly button, back to her chest, and on her neck. Whatever perfume she wore made me want to write it down to buy so much that she'd never run out. Her eyes were closed and I still had the condom in my hand. I'd unwrapped it with one hand while I played inside her with the other. Either she didn't hear the crackling of the wrapper or she was going to let me finish the deal.

I put the condom on, threw the wrapper to the floor, and slowly pushed in. Her eyes shot open and she gasped. I kissed her lips and stroked again. She put her hands in front of my stomach and slowly I took one in each hand, and with fingers touching hers, I moved her hands behind her head. I stroked again and she closed her eyes, biting down on her bottom lip.

I'd been through this before with my ex-girlfriend, Cherese, so I hoped I knew what worked to ease Seleste's body too. I licked around the insides of her lips and kissed her cheeks as I continued to stroke. Her body was still a little rigid so I reached up to massage her breasts. Instant ease in her frame but tight in the one area I needed her to be. Goddamn, I might beat Jermaine and Cara to the altar.

Afterwards, I wanted to ask her was she okay, but she wrapped herself in the covers and went to sleep. Yes! A woman who didn't need to talk. Only problem was that I liked to cuddle and she was way too comfortable with the covers. I reached for her and she rolled over and propped one leg on me. Suddenly, she opened her eyes and raised the covers slightly. She sat up and looked around the room.

"What are you looking for, babe?" I asked her lazily. I tried to reach for her again but she scooted away. That was alarming. I hoped she wasn't going to say this was all a mistake.

"Your sheets are wet," she whispered bashfully.

"That's expected. I'm the cherry popper," I said, laughing.

"I'll buy you new sheets," she said, still sitting up.

"Girl, I'm not worried about these sheets. I can buy new sheets. I can't buy another you," I said and reached over to kiss her. She moved away and jumped out of my bed.

"Here we go again," I muttered. In a louder voice, I said "Seleste, where are you going?"

She put her hands over her private areas and said, "To the bathroom." She scurried out of my bedroom and I chuckled at her hiding her body from me. It was way too late for that. I heard the toilet flush and water run. After a couple of minutes, I didn't hear her feet coming to me, so I stood up. Before I could walk out of my bedroom, this fool came in wearing a robe.

"You're kidding me," I said, with a stunned expression. Instead of answering me, she looked down at my dick. Her gaze became a stare and a look of confusion crossed her face.

"Man, are you related to horses or what?" she asked, still gawking at me.

"Silly girl, get back in this bed," I said and chased her. I snatched the robe away from her body and she ran under the covers and rolled over so the sheets looked like a dress. I eyed her frame through the sheets and felt myself rising again. I grinned at her and put my hands on my waist. Let her get another good look before round two. I walked over to the bed, she reached her arms out to me, and I paused for a second, enjoying that she wanted to be near me. In that moment, I figured out what it was that I liked about Seleste so much. In the most intimate moment, she wasn't afraid to be herself.

*   *   *

I woke up the next day and smelled something not quite familiar but it made my stomach growl. I reached over to touch Seleste but her side was empty. I stood up to put my houseshoes on and went to the bathroom to brush my teeth, wash my face, and take a piss. After I washed my hands, I went to the kitchen to find a fully-clothed Seleste in a different outfit. I walked up behind her and kissed her neck.

"What are you cooking?" I asked her.

"Tofu scramble and pancakes with soy milk," she answered, kissing me on the cheek.

I looked at the yellowish concoction in my skillet and wondered how I was going to choke that down. She covered my eyes. "Stop looking at it like that. You might like it."

"Not as much as I like you," I said. Aw, I couldn't believe I was being a sucker like this, but that's what a good woman does to you. Makes you say stuff you'd be embarrassed to tell your friends and deny to your dying day. She grinned at me and turned around to wrap her arms around me. I moved her towards me a little and away from the heat of the electric stove. "Where did you get this stuff from?" I asked her.

"I went home and grabbed some stuff. I figured you'd want something to eat before you pick your mom up." She turned around to finish scrambling the tofu and flip a pancake while my heart dropped, my dick lowered, and I landed on a nearby kitchen stool. Seleste must've felt my silence because she turned off the stove and walked between my bare legs. Since we'd gotten home last night, I'd put thoughts of the situation with my parents in the back of my mind. I'd called my godmother, Charlotte, to the hospital to be with her but right now, I started feeling the guilt of not staying with her too. Seleste rubbed my shoulders. What type of son was I to be having sex the same day that my mother went to the hospital to be tested for an STD? I jerked away from Seleste and rushed to the shower. Ten minutes later, I was showered, dressed, and headed back to the kitchen to see Seleste about to scrape the food in the garbage.

"Don't do that. You made it. Bring it with you. I'm in the car," I yelled on my way to the couch to grab my coat. I jogged down one flight of steps and started the car. She came out with two plates wrapped in a grocery bag and I sped off before she could put them on the backseat. She reached her hand out to touch my leg, and I moved away. I didn't want to tell her that I wished I was alone. Instead, I pulled in front of her house and put the car in park. She looked from her apartment to me and back again.

"I wanted to..." she started. I guess she thought better of it and slowly got out of the car. It wasn't until I'd sped off that I remembered that her car was still at my place and the food was still in my car. The smell annoyed me. I pulled into the hospital parking lot, grabbed the bag, and threw it in the garbage on my way inside. I needed to see my mother with no distractions. Seleste had already

40

clouded my mind last night, and I didn't need her to do it again.

*   *   *

"Memo, you're getting muscular, boy," Charlotte said to me when I walked in the door. She grinned and walked over to hug me. After a moment, I embraced her back. Charlotte was one of those women who was there for my mother whether she wanted to shop, gossip, or needed a shoulder to cry on. Since Terrell had been back into my mother's life, Charlotte had been pushed to the side, but she must've understood that those two needed that time to bond. Yeah, well, I see where that got her.

I looked over at my mother wearing the same clothes from yesterday. What was I thinking? I should've brought her a fresh set. Charlotte's clothes were wrinkled, so I knew she'd slept there that night. My mother let out a small smile when I hugged her.

"Memo, I have something to tell you," my mother said.

I nodded my head for her to continue.

"The doctors say that I don't have HIV." This time her grin seemed more like relief.

"But how is that possible when you said Terrell has..."

"Renee, I'm going to go to the vending machine. I'll be back, girl," Charlotte said, stepping out of the room and closing the door.

We turned our heads and waited for Charlotte to leave, and then I turned back to hear the rest of my mother's explanation. "I don't know how...well...the doctor said that I should come back in a few weeks and get tested again, but it appears I didn't get it. Terrell does have it though. He did get tested and it was positive."

"So why did you say you had it?"

41

She shrugged. "Well, he did try and did enter." She blushed a little at telling me something so private about my own father. "But I fought him. And you know, I needed to make sure. When you have sex with someone who is HIV positive, I just assumed that you got it. It only takes one pump, no matter whether you pull out or not. "

"You don't automatically get it when that happens?"

"Apparently not but the doctor told me I really lucked out because more than likely, I should have gotten it."

I wanted to be relieved that my mother wasn't going to die and Terrell was, but I wanted to make sure that the biggest crime was handled. "Did you press charges?"

Renee sighed. I waited for her to answer and she didn't. I repeated myself.

"Memo, it's just complicated. As a wife, I'm supposed to..."

"You're not supposed to be raped no matter what you are to a man," I hissed at her before she could finish. "Don't feed me that bullshit about how you're supposed to have sex with him." Her eyes flickered and I could see that the Renee who raised me and didn't take her children cursing at her too kindly was starting to show through, but I had to get into her head before her motherly tone came. "Mom, you cannot do this. You cannot give him the chance to come back around and act like this is okay. It is not okay to let a man do this to you. You didn't raise me like that, so why would you let him do this? Why do you keep giving him all of these chances?"

Before she could answer, a nurse came in. I stared icily at her for interrupting our conversation, but she continued smiling. She spoke with my mother about release papers and I looked around to make sure she hadn't left anything. Charlotte was sitting in the waiting area snacking on some type of graham bar. As soon as the paperwork was complete, I followed them both out to the car.

"Memo, I was thinking that your mother could stay with me until we get this situation straightened out," Charlotte said to me.

I shook my head. "Not happening. You have a husband and four kids. She needs peace and quiet. Mom, come stay with me. You can have my bed, and I'll sleep on the couch. I need to make sure that that..." I paused so I wouldn't curse again. "Dude doesn't come around again."

My mother looked from Charlotte to me and walked towards me.

"Okay," Charlotte said. "Well, Renee, make sure you call me whenever you want to talk. I'll be over there tomorrow to check on you." My mother nodded and embraced Charlotte, then turned to me with a worried look.

"Mom, I really wish you'd rethink this. He needs to be in jail. Either he's going to jail or I'm going. You choose," I said and started walking to my car. She followed without a word and we headed back to my place.

Suddenly she shrieked, "Where's Jeremiah?"

"He's with Arnez. I'm going to go pick him up in a little while. Why?"

"Where's he going to sleep? I don't want to be a burden."

I stopped at a red light. "Mom, you will never be a burden. Think about it. If we could stay in that small apartment in Brooklyn, we can definitely get by living in a one-bedroom apartment here. Jeremiah can sleep on the loveseat. I'll sleep on the couch. You'll sleep in my bed until you're ready to get him arrested."

"I just want this behind me."

I shook my head. "How can it be behind you when you're letting that man take over your house that you mortgaged while he was in jail?"

She pressed her head on the window. "Enough, Memo, enough. I don't want to talk about it anymore. I just want to pray because I'm blessed. I don't have an STD after all this so that's got to mean something."

I rolled my eyes and put my foot on the accelerator when the light turned green. "Yeah, it means that Terrell didn't succeed in killing you, but if you give him a chance, he'll try again." She groaned. "Like I said, Mom, it's your choice who you want to see in jail because if I see him again, I'll give you my bank access code so you can bail me out." Before she could respond, my cell phone rang. I looked down to see Arnez's cell on my caller i.d. "Fam-o, thanks for taking care of my brother, man."

"No problem. Eh, where you at? O wouldn't even tell me what was going on."

"Meet me at my spot in about twenty minutes, and bring my brother with you."

"All right. Eh, I saw your pops up in that coffee shop on the corner. I went in there to get one of those cinnamon rolls and he was at a table drinking coffee. He's looking real good these days." Arnez laughed.

My mouth dropped. A man who rapes his wife and flees the scene is too stupid not to be caught around hangout spots that my partners go to so he can drink coffee. Most folks would think a cop would have more common sense. Not my father.

"He still in that coffee shop?" I asked.

"Nah man. I walked up to him and got ready to eat my roll at his table, but he started acting all jumpy when I sat down. What the hell is going on? Before I could sit down good, he almost fell on his face trying to get out of there. Is he selling drugs again?"

I shook my head. "Nope. Worse. See you in a minute." I pressed the end button and put the phone back in my pocket. It rang again, and I saw Seleste's number. I rolled my eyes and sent the call to voicemail. I had business to attend to, and Seleste wasn't the person I wanted to handle that business with.

Chapter 7: Cara

"You should go to the hospital," I said to Seleste.

"If he wanted me to go, he'd have let me ride with him," she said.

I plugged my earpiece into my cell phone and continued to walk around the bridal shop touching different silk, nylon, and lace gowns. "Seleste, he's going through some crazy drama right now. He's just trying to make sure his mother is okay. I know he's crazy about you, but watching movies in his crib and taking care of his mother are two different playing fields." I walked to a nearby refreshment table and poured myself a cup of coffee.

"We weren't watching movies."

"You know what I mean. Whatever you two do to pass the time."

"Well, I just thought that…"

I shook a little sugar in my cup. "Hello?" I said after Seleste didn't finish her sentence.

"Yeah, I'm here."

"What's wrong? It sounds like there's more you want to say."

She cleared her throat. "Nah, I'm good."

Seleste is a terrible liar. You could see through her lies like lightning in a thunderstorm. "Did he break up with you or something?" I asked, grabbing a cookie. One of the bridal employees walked towards me but I waved her away.

"No."

I huffed, "Then what are you not telling me?"

"I'm not a virgin anymore."

My eyes widened, I reached for my coffee, and spilled it all over the tablecloth. "Shoot," I screeched. I waved at the employee who tried to help me. "Do you have paper towels?" He nodded and went towards the back area while I stopped the drink from leaking, with personalized napkins, onto the beige carpet. "Hold on," I said to Seleste. I moved the cookie plate to a nearby chair, wiped the table, and mouthed an apology to the employee when he came back with wood spray and towels. I walked around him, outside past my grandfather smoking a cigarette, and leaned against the building.

"Now, what'd you say?" I asked her.

"You heard me."

"I'm assuming Travis is the person to hit it, right?"

She groaned. "You make it sound so graphic. And yes, Memo was the one."

I whistled. "Well, now I know why you're tripping so hard. When did this happen?"

"Night before last."

"And he hasn't called you since he dropped you off at your house?"

"Nope. Jermaine took me to get my car and I didn't go upstairs to his apartment."

"Why not?"

"I didn't think he wanted to see me."

"Seleste, this is one of those times when everything can't be about you. I know your feelings may be hurt and this was a big day for you, but…it may not have been as big a day for him."

She hissed. "So I'm just supposed to act like it didn't happen?"

"No. Not at all. It's always special the first time if it's with the right person. But what made you do it now?"

"I don't know. I already knew him. We already liked each other. We talked the whole time in New York. You know, it just seemed like that time. That and I wanted to help him calm down."

"Did it work?"

"It was weird. Like that night it seemed like he put it out of his mind, but the next day when I made breakfast…"

"Stop. Hold up. My girl is growing up. You're making breakfast for brothas?"

"Shut up."

"Girl," I sang. "He must've put it on you." I laughed and saw my grandfather walking my way. "Hey, Seleste, Grandad is getting antsy. Let me hurry up and pick out a dress."

"Okay. Tell him I said hello."

"I'll do that. And you better not do anything stupid."

"I won't."

"Seleste, I'm serious. Don't assume because he's going through something else that he's not there for you. Let me know how his mother decides to handle the situation."

"Mmkay," she said.

"All right, girl. Love you."

"Love you too." We both disconnected the call. I turned to my grandfather, who was pulling out another cigarette.

"Those things will kill you, you know," I said to him.

"Before they do, I'll enjoy every minute of them," he said with a wink.

I patted him on the back and we walked inside. Although it would've been more beneficial if my mother would've come, she didn't meet us here. No surprise there. But I didn't care. My grandfather was my heart and I knew he'd help make sure I looked good. I looked over at him wearing a navy blue- and powder blue-striped shirt with navy blue slacks and shiny navy shoes. Of course he wore a navy hat to match the ensemble. I couldn't remember a time when he didn't dress like he was on a runway.

*   *   *

I gazed over at an ivory couture dress and knew it was perfect. It fit snugly around the chest, stomach, and

47

hips, and the lace branched out into a pattern with a four-foot train in the back. Sleeveless and extremely soft material. After paying the deposit, I pulled out my phone to call Seleste and tell her the news about my dress, but Jermaine's number popped up on my screen.

"Hey baby. Guess what? I found a dress."

"Cool. I know you'll look great in it. You miss me?"

"What kind of question is that?"

"You're supposed to tell me that you miss me."

"I miss you."

"You better. So are you staying out there for the next few weeks still, or did you change your mind?"

"Nope, I'm staying. I have to make sure the hall is set up correctly and my dress is fitted and all that. Did you already get fitted for your tux?"

"I'll get it done next week again. Whoever this guy you sent me to tried to make my pants into capris."

I laughed. "I'll be back the first week of May. You know I wouldn't miss the graduation."

"Three weeks without you is torture."

"Yeah right. You know it would've been more torture if I dragged you out here to help me find flower arrangements. Seleste is coming next week. I'm so excited."

"Man, you sound like you're doing way too good without me."

"Nope, I think about you everyday. This is all for you." I made a kissing noise, and my grandfather snatched the phone.

"Oh good lord, girl, get off the phone with all that gushy stuff," he said, waving the phone around. I snatched it back from him, laughing.

"Tell Cecil I said what's up," Jermaine said. "No wait, tell him I called him Pops."

I repeated Jermaine's message to my grandfather.

"If that boy calls me Cecil one more time, I'm going to really be a Pop. Pop him upside his head."

Jermaine started laughing so I knew he heard my grandfather. After a couple more minutes of conversation, I ended the call. I rolled my window down and breathed in the fresh air. "So, do you think the Louisiana people are going to make it?"

Grandad shrugged. "I don't know, punkin. They're scattered all over the place. Some of them are just trying to get back on top of their money so vacation isn't an option. You know Bush didn't do anything to help, and Condoleeza was worried about shoes."

I dropped my head, knowing if I got my grandfather on a political kick, he'd never get off of it. "And my mother?" I knew that would get him to be quiet. My grandfather had a funny relationship with my mother. She'd had me at a young age and he'd always been very disappointed with her doing so, but my grandmother had been more understanding. After she died, my mother kept her distance from Grandad. But the more she distanced herself, the closer he and I got. I think he tried to make up for the time he lost out with her by spending more time with me.

I could see him raise his eyebrow from his profile on the driver's side. "Well, you know how your mother is. She sends her best."

I bit my bottom lip and looked out at the trees. "Well, hopefully she'll come. She's going to miss something big and regret it later."

"Look at that. A doe," he said. I looked in the windshield and saw a deer run in front of the car. He braked in time, but the deer ran in circles like my grandfather was still driving. I watched her strong body pump left to right and her eyes widen as she stopped to stare at us. Suddenly, a baby deer shot out from the other side and the two immediately ran off into the trees. The mother deer was willing to risk her life just to get her baby out of the road. I guess some know how to be mothers while others don't. I looked over at Grandad and we both started humming Ray Charles song, "Georgia." It was one of those things we did whenever we saw a deer. My mother use to do it all the time too.

Chapter 8: Arnez

I stood in the financial aid line to pay my graduation fees and watched the pretty women go by. Dark ones. Light ones. Thick ones. Skinny ones. I didn't care. I would get a number just as a hobby and no intentions to call.

"Contumacious," I heard someone call out my frat name. I turned around and saw Jermaine.

"What's up, bro? How you been, Beatz?" I greeted him back, using his frat name too.

"Cara has got me running around here like I'm training for the Olympics."

I laughed. "I thought she went to Georgia."

"She did. She's got me handling things in Chicago. Did you get your tux fitted?"

I popped the collar of my fraternity coat. "I'm going to be looking more dapper than you."

Jermaine rolled his eyes and laughed. "Yeah right."

"I am. I might steal Cara back from you when I put on that suit jacket," I said, squatting down into a pose.

"Yeah a'ight. When you walk down the aisle, she's going to be like who let the dog in?"

We both laughed and I stood up to give him a handshake.

"Eh, but on a serious note, how is Memo doing? I haven't heard from him in a few days. I heard his mom didn't end up with..." Jermaine looked around and lowered his voice. "That thing."

I nodded and lowered my voice too. "Yeah. I'm happy for her, but you know his father skipped town though, right?"

Jermaine's eyes widened.

"Yeah, Memo told me when she checked her bank account, there was a charge for a plane ticket on there. His dumbass wasn't even swift enough to use cash."

"Where'd he go?"

"Probably back to Brooklyn. Where else is he going to find a place to camp out at? He knows a bunch of people there."

Jermaine shook his head. "Renee still won't press charges, huh?"

"Nope. Memo forced her into getting divorce papers though. I don't understand that. I know marriage is supposed to be for better or for worse, but it can't get any worse than this."

He shrugged. "There are some unwritten rules though. I can't believe dude did that."

I raised an eyebrow. "I can. Every time I'm around him, I just get a bad vibe. I don't trust him. The most we ever did was give each other head nods."

"How is Jeremiah doing?"

"Memo told me not to tell him, so as far as Jeremiah is concerned, their relationship just didn't work out."

"Are they still staying with Memo?"

I shook my head. "Nah, she moved back into her house about a week later. Dude bought the plane ticket the same day that I brought Jeremiah back. She got a restraining order on him though. Jeremiah is staying with Renee again in case he comes back."

Jermaine smacked his lips. "What is Jeremiah supposed to do? That boy backs out in a fight every time we're even playing with him."

I nodded. "Yeah, but dude got a little more aggressive now that he's in jujutsu classes. I don't know why Renee wouldn't just let me teach him how to fight. Or you. Memo gave up on him a long time ago."

"Yeah, because I'd be showing him a little bit of this." Jermaine acted like he was about to sucker punch someone. "And a little bit of this." He raised his boot up and stomped the wooden floor.

"Okay, but what about this?" I raised my knee and bent an invisible person across it.

"Wait, remember this move?" Jermaine said and posed in a pledging stance.

I grimaced and shook my head. "Damn, I'm glad I'm done with that. I don't even get into that with the new pledges. I leave all that hazing shit for the rest of the bruhs. I'm not trying to go to jail over somebody trying to cross, know what I mean?"

"Ummm…excuse me," a woman's voice said. "Can you take your aggression out somewhere else?" Jermaine and I turned around to see a gorgeous, dark-skinned female a little shorter than me behind the financial aid desk. I grinned wide.

"I'd rather take my aggression out on you," I said to her.

"Shee-it, me too," Jermaine mumbled. "Damn, I wish Cara was here. Anyway, fam, I'm going to let you handle that. I got to go."

I gave him dap and stepped to the desk, reaching over it and grabbing a post-it. "Write your number down before I change my mind," I said, sliding a pen to her. Before she could respond, I turned back to Jermaine, who'd walked a few feet away. "Eh, Beatz, me and Memo are going to O's house at about seven tonight. You coming?"

Jermaine turned and yelled, "I got to go taste cake. I'll meet you after that."

"What you talking about? I want to eat cake."

"Well, come with me then. All of y'all meet me at my apartment. We can eat some wedding cake and go back to O's house after that."

"Okay, I'll let them know." I turned back around and snatched the blank post-it note away from the lady. "It took you too long to think about it." I handed her my check for the graduation fees. "I could've used this money for our date."

She rolled her eyes and walked to a file cabinet to get my folder. I watched her slim frame lean over and I almost salivated looking at her C-cups. She saw me looking and crossed her arms over her chest.

"Now how are we going to get anything accomplished if you got your arms folded?"

"Stop staring at my chest then," she said, rolling her neck.

I rolled my neck right back at her. "Stop looking that sexy then." I winked at her, and her frown softened. She pressed a few buttons on her computer keyboard and printed out a receipt. She reached under the desk and handed me a plastic case with a graduation gown, hat, and a certificate case. I turned around to leave, and felt her hand on my shoulder. I turned back around and saw a bright orange post-it on my jacket. Peeling it off, I looked down to see a phone number and the name, Jackie, matching her nametag. I smirked at her and walked away.

*   *   *

"So Cara isn't going to trip if we get a stripper, right?" I asked Jermaine before I picked up another plate of cake.

Jermaine shook his head. "Are you serious? Knowing Cara, she'll want a joint stripper party. You know how she is." At the thought of her name, Jermaine pulled his phone out of its clip.

Memo made a whipping noise. "Can't go ten minutes without calling her again."

Jermaine started dialing. "Watch yourself, bruh. I saw you check your phone about eight times since we've been here, and your mother already called."

I laughed out loud. "Oooh, he got you. Who are you looking for phone calls from, Memo?"

We all looked over at him. He turned to one of the bakers. "So you said this was lemon white cake, right?"

The baker came to our table. "Yes sir, it is lemon white cake." He pointed to four other plates. "Cinnamon cake with butter frosting. Coconut pineapple cake. Coconut cream cake. And that one is carrot cheesecake." Before he could point to the third one, Jermaine walked off to another area to talk on the phone.

I shook my head. "We came to taste cake for this fool and he's on the phone."

"That man is in love. Leave him alone," O said, reaching for a square of coconut pineapple cake. "He can stay on that phone for the rest of the night as long as they don't start charging me for eating this stuff."

I turned to Memo again. "So what's up with Seleste? Why aren't you two talking?"

He shrugged. "Nothing is wrong with us. She's just being Seleste."

"And that means?" O said in between a mouth full of dessert.

"Nothing," Memo said and stood up to go in the opposite direction of Jermaine and us. I looked over at O, shrugged, and started scooping up pieces of cake onto one plate.

"What's up with the take-out plate, dawg?" O asked.

"I got a date later," I answered.

"Why do you need the cake?"

I made a face at him. "Damn, O, been that long since you got some?"

He stuck his middle finger up at me and I continued making a leftover plate. The baker saw me and he walked over. "Sir, did you want me to wrap that up for you?" I shook my head no. "Well, here's our business card if you ever want to buy a cake with us on your special day too."

O snickered. "On his special day? The day Arnez gets married is the day I say I'm gay."

"Or the day you graduate," I shot back at him.

"Aw, you're wrong for that one. I'm graduating in December."

"I don't see any proof of that."

Before I knew it, O had picked up my plate of cake and smashed it in my face. The baker started ranting about our behavior, but I wasn't trying to hear him. I wiped some of the cake from my face and smacked O across the face with it.

"I can't take y'all nowhere," I heard Jermaine say as he came running over. The baker was still hollering about O and I as we kept flinging cake back and forth, and Jermaine tried to calm him down. Memo came over to see what all the commotion was, and O took off out of the door. I chased him outside laughing, and we both headed to Jermaine's car. I looked down at my button-down to see if it was cake on it, but luckily it had only fallen onto the t-shirt I wore underneath. I buttoned one of the top ones to hide the coconut stain and looked myself over to make sure I still looked presentable. Hell did I care. I didn't know Jackie that much anyway. I was just trying to dig her out and move to the next broad.

Jermaine and Memo came charging out of the door, and Jermaine was swearing all the way to his car. "What is y'all problem? We're not in elementary school anymore. Bunch of assholes. I can't take you two anywhere. Now how am I going to explain this to Cara?"

I looked over at O and we both nodded. He walked from one side of the car and I walked from the other with our arms out. Before Jermaine could stop us, we bearhugged him, rubbing cake from our shirts and face to his. He tried to wrestle away and we hugged him harder. Memo was too busy laughing to help him and we finally let Jermaine go. I ducked when he swung on me but he caught O in the stomach.

O touched his stomach and looked at Jermaine.
"Does that mean we can't be in the wedding now?"
Jermaine tried to look serious but before he could control it,
a chuckle escaped.

Chapter 9: Seleste

I saw him standing at the bus stop and pulled over. I knew it was Jeremiah from the way he slumped and his African flag coat. No matter what the weather was, he always had that red, black, and green windbreaker with him. When I first met him, he use to wear these wristbands but I guess he upgraded his cultural pride. He also had dreads, but he'd cut them all off and replaced it with a Caesar haircut. When his hair was dreaded, it was very coarse, unlike Memo's curly hair. I always wondered if they had the same father. Even though Jeremiah's eyes were hazel while Memo's were chocolate brown, Jeremiah was much slimmer than Memo, and he was the shade of a chocolate candy bar while Memo was more like a vanilla wafer. They both had the same curly eyelashes, wide nose, and semi-arched eyebrows. Personality wise, I have no idea where Jeremiah got his from because Renee was a tough, play-no-games woman, Memo had too many personalities to be a Scorpio, and from what I'd heard from Memo about Terrell, I knew Jeremiah and his father didn't get along well. Jeremiah was one of those boys you'd see on the playground that you'd hate to walk away from for fear that the other kids would pick on him. When he got older, I was convinced he'd be the lover, not a fighter type, but right now he was just the wet type.

I rolled down my window a little so the rain wouldn't get on my seats and yelled at him leaning against the left inside area of the bus shelter.

"You want a ride?"

He peered at me and then suddenly recognized my car. I unlocked the passenger side door and he climbed in.

"What's up, Seleste? I haven't seen you in awhile." He turned my radio station to another more mainstream station.

"Look at you, getting all comfortable in my car two seconds after being in it. And please tell me I don't have to listen to this trash all the way home," I said.

"What do you mean trash? You don't like him? This song is all over the charts," Jeremiah said in shock. He started singing the words to some dumb song about how big somebody's rims were and how much money the rapper was making.

I rolled my eyes and got into the left lane. "I remember when hip hop had a point. When folks were talking about uplifting a community and current events, not just how big their house was or how many chicks they're humping." Jeremiah groaned. I laughed out loud thinking of how my own parents told me that the hip hop generation wouldn't have oldies, we'd just have fight rally songs. "I sound old, huh?" I looked at him, and he nodded with a grin on his face. "Whatever." I muffed his head and turned a corner. "Wait, am I dropping you off at your brother's house or your mother's house?"

"You're already headed to my mother's house, but I was going to my brother's house to pick up a video game."

I paused. After Memo hadn't called me for about a week, I'd left it alone. I never called him because I didn't want him to think I was one of those women who suffocated a man after she slept with him, but it's hard to not catch feelings when you've done something like that with someone. Especially the first someone. "Okay. I'll drop you off in front of the house. Does he know you're on your way?"

Jeremiah shook his head. "I have a key, so I was just going to go in there and come back out. But I'll call him." He reached on his side to pull out his cell. After dialing the number, I could hear a male voice on the other end. "Yeah, it's me. I'm on my way over there." Pause. "To get that game." Pause. "No, you don't have to come get me. Seleste saw me on the bus stop and..." Pause.

"Yeah, she's with me. She's going to drop me off at your apartment." Longer pause. "No, I have a key. You don't have to meet me back at..." Pause. "Okay." Long pause. "All right. Bye." He turned to me. "Memo said he's headed back to his apartment now. I don't know why he's got to come back. I have a key. I told him that. He must want to see you." Then he turned the radio volume up and rapped along to the next song. When I pulled in front of Memo's apartment, Jeremiah took his seatbelt off and looked at me. "You aren't getting out of the car?"

I turned the key in my ignition from running the engine to just the radio and chewed the inside of my left jaw for a couple seconds. "Nope," I finally said. Jeremiah looked at me strangely and then put the hood of his coat on and ran out of the car. "I'll wait for you to come back out," I yelled after him. He waved and ducked inside. I changed the radio to a better station and started reciting a song from an underground station. Before I got ten words out, I could see Memo's car pull up in front of me and parallel park. I watched his 5'11, basketball player frame get out of the car and he pulled his white hoodie over his head, hiding his chiseled jaw line. Even if he wasn't in the car, I'd know it was him from his bowlegged walk in his oversized jeans. I tried to fight the smile on my face as he walked to my car and opened the passenger side door.

"Better lock your doors in this neighborhood," he said, sitting down.

"Why are you in my car?" I asked.

"Girl, you better gone with that." He reached over to try to kiss me. Instead, he kissed the inside of my palm as I raised my hand to block him. "It's like that?"

I shook my head. "I haven't heard from you in like a week and a half. I should be asking you the same question."

He sighed and opened the door again. I didn't want him to get out of the car but I knew I had to stand my ground or he'd continue to think that it was okay to just leave people in the dark, mainly me. He raised his butt from the seat as one foot hit the ground, then he thought better of it and went back to sitting position with the door closed. He turned and looked at me. "Seleste, you know about the situation here. It's just been crazy. I'm not trying to say that I didn't think you were worth calling, but I just had other things on my mind."

I knew it. He was going to try to feed me with guilt. I nodded but didn't reply.

"So, I'm sorry about that. I didn't mean to leave you like that at the hospital that time though. I forgot you drove to my house, so I thought I was...well, I just wanted to see my mother on my own. That whole situation is just not something that people go through everyday."

"So how is she handling the news? Did they give her medicine?"

"She doesn't have it," he said, scratching his hair under his hood. "She thought she did because he tested positive for it, but her doctor said she's good. She wants my mother to come back again to be checked, but it looks like she lucked out."

I nodded, thinking of the irony of how Memo thought Renee was lucky.

"She didn't leave him though even when she found out. I would've left. She wanted to get him treatment but that...he acted like he couldn't wait." He leaned back in the seat and turned to look out the window.

"I'm sorry about this, Memo. I don't even know what to say to something like this." I reached out to hug him and hummed the words to the song. We sat like that for a moment until I heard a loud crash of thunder.

"I need to be getting home. This rain is coming down hard." I looked at his apartment door to see if Jeremiah was coming down. "Is he up there talking to your mother?"

"She went back home. I still go over there all the time because I keep thinking he's going to come back. By the way, he went back to New York. Who he's staying with, I have no idea. I really could care less. But she won't press charges. She claims she's going to go through with the divorce this time."

"How's she going to find him to sign the papers?"

"There's this thing you can put in the paper that says you couldn't find your spouse to divorce him. If you put an ad in the paper about it and they don't respond, within a certain time period, you can divorce them by default. One of her girlfriends did it before."

I nodded. "That's wild. Does it work?"

He shrugged. "It worked for my godmother, Charlotte, with her ex-husband. Anyway, she's at home again. That's where I just came from. But you know, back to you..."

I put a finger on his lips to shush him. "No need to explain. I understand."

He took my finger off of his lips and put his fingers through mine. "So are we good?"

Before I could answer, Jeremiah jumped in the backseat. "You should lock your doors, Seleste. Somebody could rob you if you don't."

I looked from Jeremiah to his brother. "You two are so much alike." Memo looked in the backseat at the mini-version of him and grinned. Even though Jeremiah was his brother, Memo seemed like more of a father to him. It could've been because Terrell was too busy with the police force and then jail, or Memo just had a natural knack for kids. Either way, I found it sexy regardless of me never wanting kids.

"You dropping me off?" Jeremiah asked me.

Before I could open my mouth, Memo interrupted. "You ain't leaving."

I smacked my lips. "Don't tell me what to do."

Memo got out of the car, quickly circling to the driver's side. I pressed the button to lock my door, but Jeremiah reached around me and pressed the button again to unlock it. I could see Memo's chipped tooth grin as he yanked open the door before I could do it again.

"Help me get her out the car," Memo said to Jeremiah, and before I knew it, I was being pushed and pulled from my ride. Rain and perm doesn't mix, so I jogged up the steps and under the roof of the building, pressing my alarm button as the two followed.

Nice to be back to normal, whatever that was. When we got upstairs, Jeremiah poked my stomach. "I knew you were going to come in," he said and walked around me to go in the living room where the game system was set up. I headed to the kitchen, but Memo pulled my arm towards his bedroom. I yanked my hand away and continued into the kitchen.

"Where are you going?" he whispered to me, looking a little excited in the eyes.

I squinted my eyes at him. "Doesn't work that way, dude. You can't not call me all this time and then expect me to be open like that no matter what the circumstances are." The light in his eyes faded. "Anyway, I want to talk about what's going on with your mother."

"I don't," he said in a hushed voice.

"Why are you whispering?" I whispered to him in the same voice.

"Because..." His eyes trailed to Jeremiah sitting on the couch. "Just c'mon. I promise I won't touch you."

"You're touching me now."

"Well, no more than I am now," he said, wrapping his arms around my waist. I didn't put up a fight this time, but as soon as I got to his bedroom, I hightailed it to his desk chair instead of his bed. He rubbed his left eye with his hand and groaned. I laughed as he flopped sideways onto his comforter. "Aren't you leaving tomorrow?"

I nodded. "I'm going to help Cara with some of the decorations and get fitted for my dress. I'll be down there for about a week and then be back. Why? What's up?"

"I'm going to miss you," he said, patting the bed.

I laughed at his persistence. "You are a mess."

He slid back on the bed and patted the comforter again. I shook my head no. He nodded yes. We did this again and when I said no out loud, he sat up. "Man, you're a tease."

"I'm not a tease. I just don't want to get kicked out this time like I did the last time."

He flopped back onto the bed. "Man, didn't we go through this already? I thought this was done."

"We are done."

He raised his head. "How did you mean that?"

"How do you want me to mean it?"

"You trying to leave me?" he asked.

"Do you want me to leave you?"

"Why would I want that?"

I folded my legs Indian style in his chair. "I don't know. That whole situation just seemed strange. I felt like it was a one night stand, but I didn't want it to be that way."

"Is that why you never called me?"

"When someone leaves you in the front of your house, you kind of get that feeling that they don't want to be bothered. Did you want me to call you? What would I have said?"

"The same stuff you're saying now, but without all the break-up talk."

"Well, so are we still together?"

He rolled off his bed and threw his hoodie towards the closet. It landed perfectly in his hamper. "Seleste, there will be times when I just need to do my own thing, but I wouldn't leave you hanging like that. I never thought we weren't together because I already wanted to be with you long before you were thinking about my ass. Unless you want to break up, as far as I can see it, we're good."

A grin spread across my face before I could fight it. Enough of the tough girl stuff. I stood up and kissed him on the lips. He wrapped his arms around me and kissed me a little harder, moving his body into me. It felt good to see him.

"We're good," I said, opening my eyes.

"And plus I wouldn't leave anyway. You got some good stuff," he said, laughing.

I made a face. "You're so crass." I puckered my lips out for him to kiss me again.

He made a face back at me. "What the hell does crass mean?" He kissed my teeth when I laughed at his question. I felt his hands sliding down to my bottom and didn't move them. Instead I lifted his wifebeater and lightly scratched his back. I moaned a little as he moved some of my flipped hair and kissed my neck. He may not have known the meaning of that word, but he sure did know everything else.

*　　　　*　　　　*

"Memo, I'm going to give you the keys, but please don't mess up my car. I'm serious. I mean it," I said, holding out my keys to put in his pocket.

He rolled his eyes. "Seleste, you act like I just learned to drive yesterday. Nobody is going to mess up your precious automobile. If I bang it up, I'll pay for it."

I sighed. I needed someone to drop me off at the airport and bring my car back safe and sound. The night before, I dropped off Jeremiah at his mother's house and after a couple hours of hanging out with Renee to make sure she was all right, Memo came to my apartment to spend the night. As soon as we got there, C.C., my roommate, started hassling me again about the sublease and her boyfriend. I ignored her and instead patted our dog, Shep, a Labrador Retriever mixed with German Shepherd. While I mocked him panting his tongue out, she went on and on about how I was going to Atlanta and how she felt I should just let her sublease the place again and let her boyfriend have it, never mind the fact that I was only going to Georgia for a week. She stormed out of the door, no doubt in search of her boyfriend, Jacob, while I poured canned food in Shep's dish and refilled his water. Shep was a moody guard dog. When he didn't like you, he didn't like you, but he clung to Memo quickly. I'm a strong believer in dogs knowing when trouble is near. If Memo was good enough for Shep, then he was good enough for me. I found it amusing that Shep never took too kindly to Jacob though. Didn't know the guy much besides being my roommate's boyfriend and occasionally being a freeloader and nosey, but I wanted him out of the apartment. During my stay in New York, he'd grown too comfy in my old bedroom and moved out of his parent's house. Oh well. He was going back to stay with Mommy and Daddy because I wasn't giving up my part of the apartment and the lease was in both of our names.

The next day I hesitated again when Memo reached his hand out for my keys. I treated my car like a mother would treat her child.

"Man, I'm going to love the days when you like me this much."

I winked at him. "I already like you as much as my...well, I like you enough."

He laughed. "I'm so flattered," he said sarcastically. "You let me take your virginity, but you're worried about your car," he said, tying his boots and sitting on the edge of my bed.

"Good point. You win," I said, walking to the door.

Chapter 10: Cherese

"Does your parole officer know you're here?" I asked Terrell when I stood in front of the doorway to let him in. He shook his head. I stared at him for a minute and couldn't erase the thoughts of my ex-boyfriend, Memo, lingering around. Terrell and Memo looked a lot alike: curly eyelashes, wide nose, and the same complexion. When Terrell was released, he bypassed Memo's lanky muscular build and gained more muscle. Built more like a football player and toned. "So does Memo know you're here?" He shook his head, walked in to sit on my couch, and picked up my television remote. I stood in front of the TV. "Hey Terrell, you plan on speaking to me?"

He cleared his throat and stood up. He walked to my very small kitchen in a cramped studio apartment priced at $1300. New York prices, what can I say? I watched him pour a cup of Mudslide, the only liquor I had in my fridge, and then he belched. I turned up my nose at his impoliteness. Terrell knew where everything was in my place because he'd originally stayed with me when he was released. Renee refused to have anything to do with him at the time. My mother told me it was a bad idea to let him stay with me, but I felt sorry for him. She'd found her own place, I was looking for a roommate, and hoped that he could be it once he got on his feet. There were already enough brothas in jail. It was even sadder to see a black cop go to jail, especially NYPD, since they were crazy enough as is. Luckily, he was held in a correctional facility that locked up white collar criminals. If he'd have been in jail with the hardcore criminals, he'd be dead in no time. I couldn't have that. I loved him too much for that.

"So when were you going to tell me you had AIDS?" he finally spoke.

I blinked and asked him to repeat himself.

"You heard me loud and clear, you dirty bitch," he said, grabbing my arm and slamming me against the wall.

"What are you talking about?" Tears sprang to my eyes. He reached for me, I pushed his arm away, but he slammed me again, this time lifting my shirt a little. At the sight of seeing my stomach exposed, he yanked my shirt all the way up. I thought he was trying to choke me with my own clothes but I was too stunned to react.

"All of this beauty on a deceitful woman," he said, cupping my chest. I tried to pull my shirt down, but he grabbed my neck. Tears rolled down my face. "You should've told me you had a disease before you let me sleep with you."

I blinked and let the tears fall from my face. A few months back, Renee had come to my place to get Terrell to sign divorce papers and he'd left with her. I was pissed. I'd already lost Memo when he went to Chicago for school. I wanted to be with him, but his father was the next best thing. I'd kept in touch with Terrell during the time he was in jail. Our letters started off very friendly. But, after a man hasn't had sex in awhile and is surrounded by men, he starts to get a little less selective. I missed Memo. I went to Chicago to try to get him back, and he wanted nothing to do with me. I continued to write Terrell and before you knew it, the letters became flirtatious. A bunch of comments about how he'd raised Memo better than that and Memo was lucky to have someone like me. Terrell claimed that he'd know how to treat me better. When he came to stay with me, we had sex quite a few times, but he was nothing like Memo. Memo was caring and romantic. Terrell was rough and quick. But Terrell looked like an older version of his son, and it turned me on.

I'd only had one opportunity to sleep with Memo in Chicago and that was when he met me at a hotel after a fraternity party. But nothing happened thanks to that idiot Seleste. I hated her more than the devil. Yet another reason why I clung to Terrell. But then Renee came to New York and took my new man away. I didn't care that that was her husband. He should've stayed with me. I'd slept with a few guys in between Memo and Terrell, but used protection every time except for one. I'd slept with one of Memo's friends while I was in Chicago, but as far as I knew, he was clean. He looked clean anyway.

"Terrell, why are you accusing me of having AIDS?" I asked him.

He stared at me in shock. "Are you serious? Are you really going to act like you don't know what I'm talking about?"

He released my arm, but I was too flustered to remember I was exposed. With my shirt still bunched around my bra, I said "I don't have anything."

He cracked his knuckles and stared at my black lace bra. "Yes. You. Do." He yanked my shirt down as if he was disgusted by the sight of me suddenly. "I had to lie to my own wife and say I was raped in prison to cover myself. You gave it to me. You're the only one I was with."

I shook my head. I remembered Memo's friend clearly. Solid build. Light skinned. Low haircut. Built like a miniature version of Terrell. When I got to Chicago, I walked around Memo's campus peeking into different offices. I asked for Memo by his government name, Travis Martin. In a university that big, I didn't expect to find him, but it didn't hurt to ask. One guy was walking out of the building and he heard me asking about Memo. He said he knew him and wanted to know why I was looking for him. He and I talked all the way back to the parking lot of his dorm but he never did tell me where to find Memo. He started flirting with me a little, I thought he was cute, and figured what the hell. It had been too long. I couldn't help myself.

His phone rang a couple times and he kept calling the callers Big Brother something or other. When he got off the phone, he told me I'd have to be out in a few because he was on line and not supposed to be having sex with anybody until he crossed. That brought up the topic of women and somehow he ended up telling me about a woman he liked and how Memo was trying to take her from him. That made me jealous. When the guy tried to kiss me, I didn't turn away. That was the second time we had sex, and my mind was so far gone on who Memo was trying to pursue that I forgot to ask him to put a condom on. I did leave the second time because he had to rush to some session. Even when I left his dorm, he never asked me why I was looking for Memo. He was of no use to me anymore anyway. He invited me to a party that night to see him cross and I figured it might be a good opportunity to find Memo since I knew Memo liked to party. It wasn't until that night that Memo and I came face to face and that guy was around to see us. He kept his distance from me for the whole night, but he did talk to Memo briefly. I saw him the next day when he dropped Memo off at my hotel. I guess he figured if I could get Memo back, he'd have a chance with the woman Memo was trying to steal away from him.

I came back to New York defeated and Terrell called me soon, after saying he was getting out of prison early. I'd already agreed to let him stay with me once he was on parole.

"Terrell, does Renee know we had..." I asked him.

He glared at me. "Are you listening? I told you I told her I was raped in prison." He pulled a chair from under my kitchen table and sat down with his head in his hands. "She's my wife. She wasn't supposed to fight me."

"What are you talking about?" I asked, walking closer to him.

"What is a man supposed to do when his wife won't make love to him?" He looked at me. "It wasn't my fault you gave this to me." He looked at me. "You. This is your fault."

Suddenly, it occurred to me what he was admitting. "You raped your wife?"

He jumped up. "She shouldn't have resisted me." He pointed to his chest. "That's my wife. She should act like a wife no matter what."

"You raped her," I repeated. "You raped your own wife? You're a rapist?"

"For the record, no, I didn't. Whoever said men are stronger than women lied because Renee is stronger than she looks." He kneeled in front of me. "On the other hand, you are a murderer. You gave me AIDS."

I shrunk away from him. "You can't prove that."

"You'll get tested," he demanded.

"I won't," I shouted. Before I could stop him, he dragged me to my twin bed in the living/bedroom and pinned me down. I tried to scream, but he smacked me hard across the face.

"You tell anybody I'm here, and I'll tell Memo what we did. You'll never get him back," he hissed at me.

"But I didn't..." I started to say.

Terrell held my wrists tighter. "Guess who his new girlfriend is?"

My eyes narrowed. Seleste claimed that she and Memo were together while she was in New York, but I already knew Memo was terrible at long-distance relationships. I'd glared at her the entire three months that we'd sat in a two-person office of the law firm.

"Terrell," I said slowly. "I'm going to get tested." He loosened his hold on my arms slightly. "And if it's negative, you have to leave my home."

"And when it's positive?" he asked.

I could smell his cologne. It struck me strange that even with drama like this going on, he still managed to dress well, in a khaki suit and my favorite man's cologne.

"If it's positive," I said, emphasizing the *if*, "I won't tell anybody that you're here."

"If it's positive, you and me are going to fuck. I'm getting some pussy out of this deal after all the drama." He rolled off of me and laid on the bed. I stared at his back with disgust and wondered how someone could think of sex at a time like this, but this was typical for Terrell. Everything about him was brutally honest and bossy. He turned to his side, and I felt his shoulder pressed against mine. He still smelled like the same cologne since I'd last seen him. At one point and time, I enjoyed the fragrance, but now, I wanted it off of my sheets. I'd never let anybody know Terrell was here because I knew Terrell would be true to his word and tell Memo what happened between me and his father. Memo's friend had given me his phone number, and I'd kept it in my jewelry box. I never had intentions of calling him. But if I really did have it, I wanted him to know.

"Who are you calling?" Terrell asked, yanking the phone from me.

"Pizza delivery," I lied. Terrell sucked his teeth and nodded his head mischievously.

"I haven't been off the force that long and I ain't been in Chicago too long to remember that nobody delivers in this neighborhood. Stop playing with me."

I put the phone down.

"Don't do anything stupid, Cherese," he said, watching it land on the receiver. "You tell anybody, and I go back to jail. If I go back to jail, I'm telling Memo and my wife about us. I'll have nothing to lose since they already think I ain't shit anyway."

I sighed. If that test came back positive, I was going to lose regardless. "We'll get tested together," I said.

"I was already tested. Renee made me. That's why she wouldn't sleep with me."

"Smart woman."

"That's why I married her."

*   *   *

I woke up the next day and felt a body next to me, arm wrapped around my waist. I rolled over to look into Terrell's face and yanked his arm away. I couldn't believe I got any sleep at all but the sleeping medication I took worked. If Terrell hadn't've watched me take it, I'd have downed the whole bottle and gotten myself out of this craziness. Reaching for a pair of boots, clean jeans, and a tanktop, I dragged myself to the bathroom. After showering and molding my dreads into a neat ponytail, I came out of the bathroom to see a still sleeping Terrell. No wonder he ended up in jail. He had to be the absolute worst criminal ever. I grabbed a pop tart off of my kitchen counter, knew I wasn't hungry, and put it back. I unplugged my cell phone, grabbed my keys, and jogged out of the apartment to the train headed to Nostrand Avenue. A cop bumped into me on my way in the entrance.

"You okay?" he asked.

I put my head down and walked by him without responding. With Terrell, you never knew which cops were his friends and which ones weren't. This was definitely the downside of trying to report an ex-cop. He got out of jail early from them pulling strings. I wasn't taking any chances.

I reached the doors of the facility and slowly walked in. There were posters of families and red ribbons all over the walls. There was a shot of a small black boy that stopped me cold. It was sad to see children go through something out of their hands.

"Can I help you?" I heard a woman's voice say. I turned around to look into the slanted eyes of a fair-skinned, petite woman with jet black hair and small lips.

"Yeah, I'm here for..." I looked around at the other people sitting on couches reading magazines, talking on their cell phones, and one lady bounced a kid on her knee.

The woman stood. "It's okay, miss. Everybody is here for the same thing. Please fill out this form. A counselor will be ready to see you in twenty minutes or so."

"Yeah um..." I fidgeted from one foot to the other, pulling at one of my shoulder-length dreads. "How long does it take to get the results?"

"Within a few minutes, ten at most."

I took the paperwork from the woman's hand and sat in the far right corner of the waiting area. I noticed the candy dishes full of condoms in various packaging. If you glanced at it from afar, it looked like candy wrappers.

The counselor called me into his office and I sat down nervously. He introduced himself, explaining how everything I said would be kept confidential. While he ran off a bunch of procedures about how the oral test and the blood test would be done, I recounted all the men I'd slept with. I'd known Memo since elementary school and he was my first everything, minus first kiss. When Memo went to Chicago, his friends started lurking. Some didn't want to be friends anymore, including some of his close friends. He didn't keep in touch with any of them now. They hadn't embraced him going away to college and not hanging on the block. The guys on my block loved to shoot the men down for trying to progress, but looked at the women as wife material when they were about business.

I'd only been with three or four guys during the years that Memo went away, but I thought he'd be back. The situation with him being arrested and his mother being furious at Terrell for being a shady cop made him not want to come back to visit his dad or his friends. I tried to move on. I don't think Memo thought I'd moved on though. I talked to him a few times during school but he and I both realized the relationship was strained. He came out once

74

during his junior year but I could tell he felt like a fish out of water. When I tried to be intimate with him, he turned away and the next day he left. Knowing and loving this man since eighth grade and finding out he didn't love me back struck a blow. So when he went back to Chicago, I snapped and that's when my body count went up. And they were all his friends, including the guy in Chicago. I couldn't even remember his name. That's how little he meant to me.

"Are you ready?" the counselor asked, taking out a pen and a form. I cleared my throat and nodded.

After the test was over, I sat in the waiting room until he called me back inside. When the door opened three more times, it was to let others in to get their results. They came out grinning and sashaying. I hoped I could do the same. Terrell was the last guy I was with, and when he went back to Renee, I refused to give my heart or body to anybody else. When the counselor called me back in the office with a melancholy look on his face and an apology, I knew the test came back positive before he even said it. I listened to his instructions about the doctor and hospital he wanted me to go to just to confirm that the results were accurate, but I couldn't stop the tears falling onto my cheeks.

Terrell was right. I really had given him that disease. Now he had passed it on to Renee if he really did rape her. I wouldn't say a word about him being here. If Memo found out that I was the reason that his parents had this disease, he'd come back to Brooklyn. And if he did, I knew he'd end up in jail again for trying to kill me.

Chapter 11: Arnez

I pulled into a spot on 111th street and got out of the car. Looking around to make sure none of the young wannabe thugs were looking at my truck too hard, I turned the alarm on and walked across the street to a high school track field. My sister, Corleen, went to high school here, and I use to drop her off sometimes before class. When it was off season with the football team, I'd drop her off and jog around the track a few times to keep in shape. I rolled up the legs of my jogging pants to my knees and pulled off my overcoat, adjusting the tanktop underneath. Stretching out a little at the gate, I looked around to see only two or three other people on the track. One guy racing and timing himself every few yards. Another dude jogged slowly to maintain the speed of a woman in a matching outfit.

Just as I was finished stretching, my cell phone went off. "Who's this?" I greeted the caller.

"Hello."

"Hello. Who's this?"

"You might not remember me, but I'm calling to speak with an...Arnez."

I grinned, thinking it was the lady from the financial aid office. "Is this Jackie?"

"No."

I leaned against the gate. "Speed it up then, sweetheart. Who is this then?"

"Cherese."

"Cherese? I don't know a Cherese."

"Yes, you do. Remember that party with the fraternity?"

"I remember a bunch of parties with fraternity members. I'm in a frat."

"Well, the first one."

"Look, I'm about to hang up. You're playing on the phone."

"No. Don't hang up. I need to talk to you. I'm Memo's ex-girlfriend."

I slid down to the ground slowly. Now I remembered Cherese. She was a cute, brown-skinned girl with long dreads stacked up in a ponytail. She wore all of these bracelets on her arms and had on big hoop earrings. When I saw her on campus after I'd met with my ship, I walked up to her and made a joke about how she wouldn't make any money selling incense on campus. She didn't get my joke, but she did ask me did I know someone named Travis Martin. I barely called Memo by his real name but when I recollected it, I lied and said I didn't know him. Figured it was one of his groupies trying to stalk him. I got to give it to dude. He could pull women like I could.

At the time though, I was really stressed out about one of the bruhs trying to get me to bring this girl I was messing with named Anita to a meeting. I'd just come back from dealing with that and just wanted to go to sleep. But checking out this woman with a six-pack as immaculate as mine, wearing a wraparound belly shirt that showed off her slightly muscular arms, I knew she had to look good naked. I'd turned Anita down earlier when she was trying to do something, but this girl was new cut. Wearing hiking boots and smelling like body oil, she had that mysterious thing going on. She and I walked around campus and I played it like I was helping her try to find Memo. I was a little shocked that she let me sign her into my dorm acting like Memo could've been there. He didn't even live on campus after he got kicked off the football team for fighting.

When we got to my room, she didn't hesitate to come in. My cell phone kept ringing from Jermaine calling to remind me about how we could possibly be crossing that night, but it was hard to focus on that. I'd been hearing that same speech for about a week, and at that moment, my interest was on this woman who looked more like a health club ad than a real person. I turned my phone off and got down to business. As soon as her bra came off, I put it in my bottom drawer with the rest of my collection. I guess she thought I was reaching for condoms because she looked at my bare hands hesitantly while I laid between her legs. I started dry humping her and her eyes rolled back. Forget the condoms. I wanted to be in her raw. She smelled like vanilla and some kind of fruit. After it was all said and done, I turned my phone back on and had about five messages from Jermaine and one from Big Brother Sweet cursing me out for not picking up the phone. I knew I was getting the wood tonight but I didn't even care. This Cherese woman had relieved some tension and my room smelled so good. She got up first though and quickly dressed. I gave her my phone number, invited her to the bridge that night just in case Jermaine was right this time, and told her Memo might be there. Hey, I wasn't selfish. Memo could get some of that incense lady too.

I was so charged about crossing that I didn't pay attention to Cherese walking into the party until I saw the big argument Memo and her had that went from the front room to outside. That's when it clicked that this wasn't just any Cherese; this was Memo's Cherese. No point in throwing salt on her game. Hell, he wasn't concerned about me when I was trying to get with Seleste so why should I have been worried about sleeping with his girl? Plus, if those two got back together, I knew I'd have a better chance to get Seleste. I didn't hesitate to drop him off at Cherese's hotel the next day so they could talk, since apparently O and him had dropped her off that night without coming up. She and I played it cool like we'd never met and I hadn't heard from her for the rest of the winter or spring semester up until this phone call.

"Yeah, what's up?" I asked hesitantly.

"How are you doing?"

I looked at the phone with disbelief. I knew she didn't call to check on my state of mind. "Good. You?"

"I'm all right."

Silence.

"Look, babe, I got some stuff to do. Can I call you back?"

"No," she said quickly. "Okay, I need to ask you something, and I need you to tell me the truth."

I nodded and almost laughed when I realized she couldn't see me. "Yeah," I said aloud.

"Have you ever been tested?"

"Huh? I'm graduating with Memo."

"Not that kind of test."

"Spell it out for me, boo. No time for the guessing games."

"For any diseases."

My mouth dropped. "Oh my gawd, please tell me you don't have anything."

"What?" she shrieked. "I was asking because I think you gave me something."

"No burning here. I'm good. What are you talking about?"

"You are the only person I could've gotten this from."

"Gotten what?"

"AIDS."

I looked at my phone like it had grown a head, and then I closed it. I wasn't trying to hear this. Anita had called me this past semester talking the same garbage. I never got tested for her because I didn't believe I had anything. She was a bustdown anyway. I wasn't about to let Cherese accuse me of something too. I turned my phone off and put it in my side pocket. Time to get my exercise on.

*   *   *

"Arnez, I tried to call you yesterday. I got an operator's message about your cell phone wasn't in service," Memo said. He'd called the number to my dorm.

"Yeah man, this bitch was playing on my phone so I got a new number. I just got it this morning."

"Hard out there for a pimp, huh?" Memo asked, laughing.

"You know how I do it. Anyway, let me give you the new number," I said, reaching for my phone to retrieve the new number. When I got off the phone with him, I called Jackie. I needed to get some tonight. I hope she wasn't one of those I-need-to-know-you-better females.

Chapter 12: Seleste

Cara's grandfather's car was filled with flyers all over the backseat and gift bags on the floor. I'd just left the tailor's shop to get my dress made, and we decided to go to a breakfast inn to eat. We talked about who was spending money on what between her grandfather, herself, and Jermaine until the waiter walked over to take our drink order, and we headed to the buffet table.

"So are you still staying out here until the graduation?" I asked her.

She shook her head. "I'm going to try to come back earlier than June. I miss my baby, plus I'm scared of what kind of cake he got. I want to see his suit too. Make sure he doesn't have all the groomsmen sagging their pants."

I laughed.

"Talked to Memo lately?" she asked me.

"I spoke with him last night."

"And?"

"Cara, I know it might sound petty, but I don't get why he won't tell Cherese that he's with me."

"You spend too much time thinking about that girl. She's way in Brooklyn minding her own business."

"But still...I guess with Renee's situation, I'm even more cautious with who I sleep with."

"You've only been with one guy and how many times were you even with him like that?"

"Only that one time."

Cara shook her head and walked with me back to our table. "You didn't even polish him off before you left?"

"Polish him? Girl, some of the stuff that comes out of your mouth amazes me."

"You should be more worried about what goes in it." She howled with laughter while I shook my head at her and reached for the pepper.

"Cara, let me ask you a question."

She calmed herself enough to say, "Go ahead."

"Do you ever wonder if Jermaine is cheating on you?"

Her expression turned serious. "You trying to tell me something?"

I shook my head. "No, no. Not like that. I just wonder because if Memo's parents have been married all that time, and she didn't know about his side hustle with drugs, who knows what else he's keeping from her? Hell, she doesn't even know where he's hiding out. I'm glad she tested negative and all that, but that's got to be stressing her out, not knowing if he's coming back."

Cara shrugged. "All she has got to do is report him. She chose not to. That's her problem."

"I can't believe you're trying to blame her."

Cara picked up her fork and knife, sectioning off her pancakes. "I can't sit here and act like I don't think her decision is dumb. If she doesn't report it, he has the opportunity to do it to somebody else."

"Yeah, but I guess she's scared."

"Imagine how scared the next woman will be."

"You know what I'm scared of?"

"What?"

"The fact that she couldn't trust her own man. You'll never have to worry about that with Jermaine though."

Cara nodded. "Yeah, he's a good one. I think Travis is too."

I shrugged.

"Do you even miss Arnez?"

"Hell no," she said and burst into laughter. "Not one bit. Arnez is one of those guys who will be the old man at the club and never settle down."

"Cara, I have another question for you."

"And I have another answer."

"I know you hate condoms, but aren't you ever scared of getting pregnant?"

Cara hesitated before she answered. "Not really. I want kids with Jermaine."

"But does he want kids right now?"

"No, he said he'd rather get married first and get his money right."

"So do you have unsafe sex with him?"

She rolled her eyes. "Oh gawd, is this going to be another sex education course from Dr. Seleste Venton?"

I picked at the watermelon on my plate. Cara had been eating the entire time, but I hadn't touched a thing. Talking about Renee made me lose my appetite. Cara must have seen the frustration on my face because she stuck her fork on my plate and picked up my hash brown, waving it in my face. I flicked her fork away from me.

"Why are you asking me this anyway, Dr. Venton?"

"Cara, I just don't get you. Even when a situation is this close to home, you still don't want to be more careful?"

"I know Jermaine isn't cheating."

"But what about Arnez?"

"That's in the past. You and I both know he wasn't exclusive anyway."

"But AIDS is in the present."

Cara chewed the hash brown. "I don't want to talk about this anymore."

"I do."

"Well, I'm not going to."

"Cara, Jermaine is my best friend. I think you should get tested. If not for you, for him."

"I'm your best friend too. Did you say the same thing to him?"

"Yes, but I know Jermaine does it. That's why I'm asking you."

"Seleste, it's none of your business what I do with my own body," she said, jamming bacon in her mouth.

"You kill me. You come back from New York trying to tell everybody how to live their life. Was I telling you what to do when you almost got kicked out of school for fighting Lisa over Memo? Nope. I didn't judge you, so don't judge me. And if it makes your judgmental ass feel any better, your friend asked me to get tested already."

"Jermaine?"

"Who else? You and Arnez don't kick it!"

"When did he make you get tested?"

"Last month. You want the health insurance receipt to prove it, nosey."

I sighed and rolled my eyes. "Cara, it was just a question. I don't see why you're acting so defensive. Was the test negative?"

"Of course it was negative. I knew it would be even before I found out."

"How come?"

She gulped down some of her orange juice and bit a strawberry. "I was tested after I stopped fooling around with Arnez. He'd given me something else so that was another reason I got tested."

I shook my head and folded my arms. "What'd that dummy give you?"

"A baby." She shoved more bacon in her mouth.

I blinked at her a few times and cleared my throat. "Oh my gawd. What'd you do?"

"I'll give you one guess and no lifelines," she said, picking up a piece of sausage. I stared at Cara shoving down food and it suddenly clicked to me that she was this hungry when we went to the Cheesecake Factory after I flew back home. But Cara was always hungry, so at the time, I didn't pay attention. I looked at her face and noticed that her cheeks looked a little puffier. She wore microbraids but around the sides of her head, it was a darker shade. She met my gaze and continued chewing.

"How many months are you?"

"Four."

"Does Arnez know?"

"Yup. He can't wait for Jermaine and I to get married so he can put the baby off on him."

"So, how is Jermaine taking the news?" I asked her. I couldn't believe Jermaine kept this kind of secret from me. He and I always talked about our relationships. I went to Jermaine as quickly as I went to Cara when I wanted advice. He was that kind of guy that you'd be at ease with. I wasn't surprised that Cara hadn't told me this news though. She and I had such different views on everything and usually ended up arguing when it came to relationships or sex and not speaking to each other for days.

"What he doesn't know won't hurt him," she said looking away.

I scowled at her. "You're marrying him and you're not going to tell him that you're pregnant with Arnez's child."

"Seleste, Jermaine and I were going to have kids sooner or later. Hell, if he was so worried about kids, he wouldn't have talked me out of condoms too. Just like Arnez. You know what your problem is? You're always blaming me about not using protection, but I never hear you telling Jermaine the same thing. He's just as irresponsible."

"But he can't bring a life into this world," I shouted. "I'm so tired of women blaming the man for not being responsible. We're the ones who can make the decision on the child and we're the ones who have to carry it. Grow up. You're a grown woman and nobody can tell you what to do with your own body. It's up to you."

"Lower your voice," she said through gritted teeth. I looked around to see a few people sneaking looks at us out of the corners of their eyes and one or two gawking.

"Cara," I whispered. "Regardless of you and Jermaine not being careful, he has the right to know something like this before he marries you. You can't let him believe it's his child once you start showing."

She stared at her food. "But what if he doesn't want to be with me if he finds out?"

I leaned over. "Cara, I can't keep something like this from him. Either you tell him or I will because obviously Arnez won't."

"Seleste, you keep your mouth shut or you won't be in my wedding."

I stood up and pulled out my phone. "I'll tell you what. If you don't tell Jermaine before this wedding goes down, he won't be at your wedding either."

"He'll still marry me," she said, standing up and putting her hands on her hips.

I pressed both hands against the table. "Well, if you're so sure of that, why won't you tell him then?"

She didn't answer.

"I'm going home. I'm done here." I walked to the front booth and asked the host for the yellow pages to call a cab. Before she could give them to me, I felt an arm yank mine. "Get off me," I snapped at Cara, without looking behind me.

"Seleste, why are you acting like this? I just want to tell him in my own way." I turned to glare at Cara whose eyes were watering.

"Ma'am," the host said. "I would appreciate it if you and your girlfriend would take your personal arguments outside please. I don't want to have to call a manager."

"Girlfriend?" Cara and I exclaimed. We both looked from the hostess to each other and left the restaurant. Before the revolving door could turn enough to let us both out, we were laughing.

"Aw man, I can't believe they thought..."

"That was wild," Cara said.

I looked behind me to see some people peering out the window.

"I guess they're waiting for us to kiss or something," Cara joked. I smiled at her and she smiled back, but our happiness quickly faded. "Look Seleste, for real though. I really would prefer that you not tell Jermaine about this situation. I'm going to tell him, but I just want to be in his face to do it. This is not something I would do over the phone. That's another reason why I want to go back early."

"But you have this man at home planning a wedding. What if it doesn't happen?"

"If Jermaine loves me like he claims he does, he should understand that things happen." She started walking to her grandfather's car, and I followed. We both got in, and she turned the radio on.

Before she put the car in drive, I said, "And if you love him like you say you do, you'd give him the chance to decide before he marries you."

*   *   *

"Why are you leaving early?" Cara asked.

"I hope that question was rhetorical," I answered.

"Ladies, there's no need to argue, especially with the big day coming," Cecil interrupted us from the passenger seat. I hadn't said a word about why I cut my trip short or debated with Cara anymore since we went to the restaurant. But looking at other wedding stuff wasn't nearly as fun the next day.

"But you haven't even tried on the dress again to make sure it fits. You might as well stay the whole week," she said.

"Your designer pinned me. It should be good," I said. What I really wanted to say, and if Cecil wasn't around, was if she didn't tell Jermaine what was going on, then I didn't want to be in the wedding anyway.

I could feel her staring at me so I moved from the backseat of the driver's side to the passenger side. She'd have to move her rearview mirror to see me. The rest of the ride was quiet. Cecil hummed different songs and I looked out the window. Atlanta looked like any other major city, with the billboards, restaurants, and hotels, but the trees were prettier and just about every man I saw was handsome. Even looking in the cars zooming by or keeping up with us, side profiles looked promising.

When Cara and I left the restaurant, we saw a group of guys standing outside laughing and talking with a slight drawl. Clothes matched from head to toe. Even in hip hop gear with the pants sagging slightly, they still looked neat. The gold teeth killed me, but some of them made it work. I felt bad for the women in ATL having such a larger population. These dudes were the type you wished would come over and talk to you. I shouldn't've been thinking about that, with Memo in Chicago. But who's to say he wasn't still messing around on the phone with Cherese or someone else? It wasn't like I could watch him in Chicago.

My time in New York wasn't nearly as dramatic as I thought it would be with her around. When I first set foot there, the smell of urine caught me off guard. I wondered if it was because garbage was set out front of buildings for the garbage men to pick up instead of put in dumpsters of backyards or alleys. The crowd didn't bother me too much. It was equal to walking in downtown Chicago by Union Station during rush hour on Madison and Wacker. The trains were always packed and I snapped on a couple of people for groping me, but other than that, it was cool.

Even though Cherese and I were the only interns, there were a couple of entry-level employees who were paid to run errands for the lawyers like picking up contracts, so I traveled with them as much as possible to get myself acquainted. I got to travel to different boroughs like the Bronx, Manhattan, and Staten Island, but I spent most of my time gawking at rent prices. I was set up in a building where the lawyers stayed, but I flipped through newspapers to see how much it would cost to stay. C.C. had called me several times hoping I would move so Jacob could stay, but seeing apartments almost $500 more than Chicago apartments, I turned her down on that suggestion.

One time I tried to travel alone and ended up lost. The lawyers I worked with were in a meeting and the two entry-level workers weren't answering their phones. I knew I couldn't call Cherese because she'd send me to the worst part of Brooklyn she could think of, so I dialed a number to a person I thought I could trust.

"Yeah," a male voice answered.

"Memo, I'm lost," I said.

I tried to hold back my laughter when he started singing Robin Thicke's "Lost Without You" song. "Mr. Showtime at the Apollo, are you done?" I asked.

He stopped singing. "How's New York treating you?"

"Not so good. I had to run an errand, and I can't figure out how to get back."

"Mmph, mmph, mmph. See how you are. I'd have never gotten a phone call if you weren't stranded, but it's all good. Where are you now?"

I told him the cross streets I was on, and it turned out that I was only a block away from the train that would take me back. That night when I got home from work, he called me to make sure I got back safely, and the conversations continued. When I left for Chicago, it wasn't on good terms, so he and I hadn't had the chance to really see where each other's head was at. By the end of my three months there, I was pretty sure I knew where his was.

"Earth to Seleste," Cecil said. I looked over at Cara's grandfather and saw that we'd reached the airport. They both got out to help me with my bags. Cara asked me did I want her to walk me in, I shook my head no, hugged Cecil, and gave her a head nod before turning to walk away.

"Hey Seleste," Cara yelled after I'd walked a few feet in the parking lot. I turned around to see her jogging towards me. "Don't forget that you and I were friends first. You tell him about this, and we'll be enemies just as fast."

I raised an eyebrow, cocked my head to the side, and opened my mouth to snap. I looked into her blinking eyes and could tell she was trying not to cry. Instead of debating, I turned on my heels and left her standing there.

*   *   *

"At least you brought less bags this time," Jermaine said, as he walked up to me by the exit doors.

"What are you doing here? I thought Memo was picking me up."

"Aw, see how you are? Got a man a few weeks and forgetting about your boy."

I tried to put a weak smile on my face, but I knew Jermaine would see straight through me. He looked down at me and reached out for a hug. I hugged him back and kept one arm around his waist.

"Why are you back early anyway? Where are the souvenir bags?"

"I didn't buy anything."

"Whoa, Seleste didn't shop. What happened? You and Cara were too tired to shop after she dragged you around for the wedding?"

I looked at the friendly bright grin on Jermaine's dark chocolate skin and the platinum stud in his ear. With his tall stature and muscular build, I could understand why women wanted to keep him. He had the personality to match his looks, and Cara liked him from first sight. She wore her heart on her sleeve, and he was crazy about her. Who was I to break those two apart? I leaned my head against his side and didn't respond.

90

"Uh oh, you're being touchy feelie. What happened? You and Cara got into it?"

I looked up at him and asked, "What makes you think that? You talked to her?"

"Nah, you're always really affectionate to other people when you get into it with somebody. Most folks take their anger out on everybody else. You cling to people. So what happened?"

I shrugged. "Nope. Just happy to see you."

"Sounds like there's more to it, but the police are about to tow my car if I don't leave the pick-up spot so forget it," he said, moving faster out the door with my bag.

Chapter 13: Memo

I looked around the station at police officers bringing in handcuffed, scowling men and one prostitute, who tried to flash me before a cop grabbed her. The officer at the front desk had a lackadaisical stare on his face as if he'd seen and done everything. It was the same expression that my father would have on his face when he came home from work. I'd finally convinced my mother to fill out a police report and get a restraining order against Terrell. While we waited for someone to come out and talk to my mother after the paperwork was filled out, she turned to me and touched my leg.

"Memo, I think you should get tested," my mother said to me. I rolled my eyes. I'd only been with a couple of random females between Cherese and Seleste, and I'd strapped up immediately with them. I was trying to finish school and not fall into the trap of taking care of kids I didn't want until I graduated. Jeremiah was enough of a child for me. I'd been tested every six months since Cherese. I always told my boys to do it too, but it never crossed my mind to tell my own mother. O would come with me most of the time, and Jermaine rolled with us too, but Arnez would never go.

His response was always, "If I have it, I don't want to know. And if I don't have it, even better." It wasn't like I was messing with him, so I didn't care.

"I'm good, Mom. I take care of me," I responded.

"What about that girl?"

"What girl?"

"The one who came to the house with you."

"Seleste?"

"I forgot her name. You were the one bringing all of those people in my house. She was the only woman who came with you that day too."

I repeated Seleste's name.

"Watch her. Make sure you get her tested."

"Who said I was doing something with her?"

My mother made a face at me. "Memo, don't forget that I'm a woman first. That girl came in my house like she was ready to do battle before you could. You brought her to your momma's house, and she was the one on that porch following you around. It doesn't take a genius to see that she cares about you. And you are your father's child. You two are doing something."

I gritted my teeth at her for comparing me to Terrell and shook my keys. "I'm out of here, Mom. I'll be in the car if you need me." I leaned over and kissed her on the cheek, but she yanked me down to the seat.

"I need you now. I'm sorry. I promise I won't compare you to him again," she said. I looked at her and leaned back against the wall. She tied the straps of her sweater around her waist and shivered a little, leaning back on me. It was about eighty degrees outside, and with the blue jeans and short-sleeved, button down I had on, I was almost baking. I considered taking off my top shirt and just wearing the wifebeater, but the more uncomfortable she looked and the ice cold stares of the people who were arrested, the more I started to get chilly. It was strange. I'd never thought twice about the guys I grew up with going in and out of jail nor did I pay much attention to the cops my father brought over for dinner or hung out with. Even working in the same office as the parole officer, I didn't stop to wonder what the guys and women going in and out of there did to be put on house arrest. But with my mother being the attacked, I was looking at the police station with new eyes. I wondered how long it would take before she stopped overdressing. Summer was around the corner.

I opened my arms to hug her, and she leaned closer to me. I couldn't imagine somebody wanting to harm her. I wish I knew where Terrell went. Thought about calling

Cherese to see if he'd gone there, but if I did that, she'd know my cell phone number, and I'd have to deal with her blowing up my phone trying to rekindle a dead relationship. She had my home number though, and I knew she'd call me if she saw him.

I wanted to contact my boys in Brooklyn but the last time I went out there, all I got was a bunch of snide remarks about going to college. I knew that even if Cherese didn't see him now, she'd pass the word to them and they'd let her know.

"Memo, can I ask you a question?" my mother said, interrupting my thoughts.

"Mmm hmm."

"How did you feel about the situation with Jeremiah? You know, when your father and I first started having problems."

I raised my eyebrow at her wondering where this question came from.

"I never told you this, but that was the real reason I took him back after he was released from prison. I knew that he was up to no good on the police force, and I tried to leave him. I just wanted to see what it was like to not be with him. I never planned to have Jeremiah, but I love that boy to death and don't regret what I did. Terrell forgave me for doing what I did, and in turn, I ignored some of the things I heard about him doing while he was a cop. But I always wondered why you've never even asked me about Jeremiah's father before."

I shifted in my seat and clapped my hands together. "Mom, I really don't ask questions that I don't want to know the answer to. I know sooner or later you and Jeremiah are going to have to sit down and talk about his father and why he bounced, but I really feel like that's between you and Terrell."

"Do you think I deserved what happened to me? You know because I cheated on your father."

I reached out for my mother's hands. "Mom, you got to know better than that. No matter what happened between you all almost thirteen years ago, you still never deserved to be raped. You raised me to respect women and so did he. I don't know why he did what he did, but don't ever think it was your fault. Okay?"

Before she could respond, an officer walked up to us. She stood up and followed the officer, but then turned to look over her shoulder at me. I mouthed, "I'll be right here." When she disappeared from my view, I put my earpiece in and pressed the speed dial number to call Cherese. The phone rang a couple times, and I heard someone pick up.

"Did you do it?" a muffled voice said.

"Hello?" I looked at my cell to make sure I'd dialed the right number. I heard heavy breathing and no answer. "Sorry about that bruh, I must have the wrong number." There was a long pause and then the dial tone. I deleted the number from my phone and got ready to dial her mother's house. It never occurred to me that she could've changed her cell number. While I was searching for her mother's number, the cop who came for my mother whistled to me and waved me in his direction. I closed my phone and took my top shirt off. It was hot again.

*   *   *

"I sure do know how to pick them, huh?" my mother said as we got back in the car.

"Mom, don't start blaming yourself. Terrell got caught up in the game and just started to wild out," I responded.

"English, boy, English."

"Dad was looking for easy money and he found it. But he also found an easy way to jail. Twice."

"I still can't believe I didn't end up with the disease. Who thinks about stuff like that when they're married? I

95

was supposed to be safe. Those men who raped him
should be dead."

"It ain't like the guard is going to hand him a
condom. Guards know what goes down in there. They
should be locked up for letting it happen."

"Maybe the guards don't know."

"Mom, please. If they know when someone is
trading cigarettes, they know when somebody is getting
raped."

"The screaming."

"The crying."

"And fixing them up the next day. You know it's
funny. I didn't see any marks on that area of him. Shouldn't
it leave a mark?"

I turned the radio on. "New subject. The last thing I
want to talk about is Terrell's butt."

"Why do you keep calling him by his first name?"

"I call him dad too."

"You call him Terrell more. You've been doing that
since he went to prison. It's like he's not your father."

I turned the volume dial to make the music louder. "I
wish he wasn't." I thought the music was loud enough to
block me out, but the look of remorse my mother gave me
told me she heard me loud and clear.

*   *   *

I laid down on my couch and pulled out my phone to
dial Cherese's mother's number, but my phone lit up to
show an incoming call from Seleste. I'd forgotten she was
back in town that same day, especially when my mother
called me that morning and finally agreed to go to the
police station. I called Jermaine to ask him to pick Seleste
up and left. After my mother and I came back from the
station, we went to the hardware store and changed all of
the locks. Jeremiah walked in the house in the middle of

me doing this and I handed him a spare set of keys. He asked me how Terrell was supposed to get in when he and my mother made up. I looked over at my mother, and she guided Jeremiah to the kitchen to talk. By the time I left, Jeremiah was locked up in his room. I'd planned on calling him to see how he was doing as soon as I got confirmation from Cherese that Terrell wasn't there. I pressed the talk button. Seleste and I talked briefly about her flight. She wouldn't tell me why she came home early but that was a typical Seleste move. Her and Cara probably got into it about something stupid and would be talking before the day was out. We made plans to meet up later and when I hung up the phone with her, Arnez called.

"What's up, fam?" he greeted me.

"Regular. I finally got my mother to go to the station. She changed her locks and told Jay what happened."

"How'd he take it?"

"He's locked up in his room not talking to anybody. You know how Jeremiah is."

"Terrell is going to send that boy to therapy."

"I know right."

"Anyway, I was calling to see if you wanted to chill with me and these two girls."

"Like a date?"

"Yeah. I'm diggin' one of the girls out though. She's fine as hell. Works in the financial aid department. If she ever gives that job up, she can make some nice money giving head."

I laughed. "You're wild, dude."

"I'm just saying. It's the truth though. This one is an expert."

"Anyway, nah, I don't want to go."

"Why not? You got something to do?"

"You thought I was lying when I said I was with Seleste? No, I'm serious. She's not having that."

"Who said I was going to tell?"

"You don't have to tell anything that's not happening."

"Well, I guess that's more for me."

"Enjoy."

We hung up the phone and before I could dial Cherese's mother's number again, my mother's number appeared.

"What's up, ma?" I answered.

"It's me, Jay," I heard Jeremiah answer.

"Aw okay. What's going on with you, bruh?"

"Why didn't you tell me?"

I switched from the right side of my couch to the left. "I wanted Ma to tell you what happened in her own time."

"Not that. Why didn't you tell me about Cherese and Terrell?"

Chapter 14: Jermaine

I parked my car by the dog beach and headed towards the boats by Irving Park, walking past people barbecuing, walking dogs, and lying in the grass and hammocks. The lakefront was one of my favorite ways to relax, and it reminded me of why I came back to Chicago when my deejaying job in California didn't work out. Cara was talking about moving to Atlanta once I graduated, and I was thinking about it. The music scene was definitely stronger there than in Chicago lately, but I would miss it if I left.

The southside of Chicago was heavily populated with Blacks and the northside was a little more diverse, with Jamaicans, Africans, Mexicans, and Middle Eastern people walking down the same blocks and living in the same apartments. The club scene was better too. I'd get a larger audience when I deejayed at random clubs that played all kinds of music. Always partial to the hip hop pioneers, though, like Big Daddy Kane, Kool Moe Dee, MC Lyte, Queen Latifah, Melle Mel, and Ice Cube of NWA. I adjusted the volume on an old school, hip hop track blasting through my headphones and jogged the rest of the way to the boating area.

In May, the boats started coming out heavier and runners and bicyclists would see the people who fished increase. I use to come this way with Seleste when we were younger, but she was forever complaining about people killing fish, so when I was introduced to Cara, I started bringing her. The wedding plans were stressing me out, so I knew it had to be getting to Cara too because I hadn't heard from her in about a week. She was supposed to be back in mid-May because she'd finished everything up until I got there and with the music gigs I was doing, we were both crazy busy. I was in the middle of sending her a text message to see what was up with her when a female sat next to me on the bench. I glanced over and immediately recognized her profile. Anita was one of Arnez's many fans in college. She was also head of the cheerleading squad and the muscular legs under her short khaki shorts displayed just that. She'd been the reason that Cara and Arnez stopped messing around too, and for that reason alone, I liked her.

"Jermaine?" she said, peering at me trying to see past the sunglasses and my headphones.

"Yeah, it's me, Anita. How you been?"

She scooted a little closer. "I'm good. You?"

"Real good. Just came here to chill."

"Yeah. You come here often?"

"Not as much as I'd like too, but just trying to stay in shape."

"Me too."

I couldn't help my eyes from traveling back to those legs. "You're doing a good job." She grinned at me. Maybe I shouldn't have said that. Anita was nowhere near selective when it came to sex. I didn't want to be her next target for that reason alone. Just because a man can have it doesn't mean he always wants it, unlike what most women think.

"I heard you're engaged to Cara," she said, looking me over. Anita had a way of making a man feel like he was naked even when he was clothed. But I was even more of a target since I'd taken off my wifebeater while I was running and it hung out of my back pocket. No shirt. Just baggy, knee-length khaki shorts and gym shoes dirty from debris along the bike path.

"I am," I said. "Can't wait to marry her. That's my baby."

She frowned at that last comment. "So how is your boy Arnez doing?"

I nodded. "Good." I didn't want to say too much about Arnez. From his standpoint, Anita use to blow up his phone after they stopped messing around. He talked to her a lot before then, but not so much within the past semester.

"I don't see how," she mumbled.

My left eyebrow raised. "What did you mean by that?"

"You don't know?"

"Know what?"

"About his situation?"

I took my sunglasses off. "What situation are you talking about?"

"That fool never took me seriously. I told him to go to the doctor. You mean to tell me he didn't?"

I pulled the headphones down to my neck. "Anita, what are you talking about? Did something happen to Arnez?"

"Yeah, and he passed it to me."

"What'd he do? Burn you?" I wouldn't put it past Arnez to do it.

She squinted her eyes at me. "You really don't know, do you?"

I frowned. "Know what? Just tell me what you're talking about."

She shook her head. "Never mind. He'll tell you in his own time, but you better hope he deals with it before it turns into full blown..." She covered her mouth. "I got to go." I reached out to grab her, but she took off running along the circle path towards the stair pathway where the fishermen sat on. Whatever. Anita was always trying to keep up some drama. I wasn't trying to listen to her.

*　　　　*　　　　*

An hour later and with a cramped back from sleeping so long, I sat up and got ready to walk back to my car when my phone rang. It was Arnez needing a jump for his truck. He'd hung out late last night and forgot to turn his lights off. I told him I'd be there in about an hour or so, and he said he'd meet me in a mall near Cicero. I asked him why didn't he ask Memo to meet him since he was closer, and found out Memo was at his mother's house again. By the time I got to Arnez, he was outside talking to some woman with a cell phone in her hand. I stepped back and let him do his thing until he saw me. He hurried over after she walked away, and I handed him the jumper cables to give his truck some juice. When he was done and I placed my cables into the trunk of my car, I got ready to get back inside but stopped and turned to him as he was walking to his car. "Eh, Arnez, guess who I saw today?"

"Who?" he asked, lifting one leg up to climb inside of the SUV.

"Anita."

He turned his lip up in disgust. "Did you run?"

I smiled. "Nah, but I should have. You know she's always trying to start some stuff. She didn't have her friend Lisa with her though."

"We could just sic Seleste on her."

We both laughed at that one. "Yeah. She had some crazy stuff to say about you though. Trying to say you gave her something."

"I did give her something. Some of this good dick."

"You know she lied and said you gave her more than that though."

His smile got a little tighter. "What did she say?"

"You know what? Never mind. It's not even my place to say something about it."

"Naw, tell me what she said."

"Okay, but hey, what happens between you and her is between you and her. The only reason I'm wondering is because you and I both know that you use to mess with Cara so I just want to look out for my fiancée."

"No doubt. But what did she say?"

"She didn't really tell me what it was you gave her. She started getting all mysterious on me, but Anita is usually the first person to start some gossip up so it seemed kind of weird that she didn't want to finish it off."

Arnez shrugged. "You know how that girl is. Forever trying to act like she's on a soap opera. Just ignore her."

I nodded my head at him, but my stomach started to knot up a little. He leaned against the hood of his car and averted eye contact by looking at the cars speeding by. Arnez was crazy about cars and always yelling at somebody to get off of his, so something like leaning on someone's car wouldn't be a big deal for anybody else to do, but from him, I knew something was wrong. He regarded his truck like a parent would regard their child. He was forever washing it, polishing it, and adding something new to it. "Something on your mind, bruh?"

He shook his head but didn't make eye contact. "Nah, I'm good."

I stared at him for a minute and slowly slid into the driver's seat. "All right, well, I'll be talking to you then."

He cleared his throat and turned his back to me. No thank you for coming all the way there. No dap. No jokes. Nothing. Yeah, something was wrong. I plugged the earpiece into my phone and called Cara. The phone rang a couple times and she answered groggily.

"What's wrong, babe?" I asked.

"Nothing," she mumbled. "I'm just a little sick. Maybe coming down with a cold."

"In Atlanta with all that nice weather? That's messed up. I know the weather has to be beautiful."

"Yeah, I guess."

I started my car and reversed in the mall parking lot I was in. "So what's up?"

"Not much."

"Wow, nothing to say to me after not talking for a whole week? I figured you'd be talking my ear off about the wedding."

"You could've called me too."

I made a face at the phone. "Are we about to start arguing because if that's the case, I'm hanging up. I don't need three people acting weird in one day."

"Is one of those three Seleste?"

"Surprisingly not."

"Have you talked to her lately?"

"Not since I picked her up from the airport."

"Oh." Pause. "So what'd you talk about at the airport?"

"Same ole, same ole. You know how Seleste is."

"What do you mean by that?"

I waved at a driver to thank him for letting me cross through traffic to get to the opposite lane. "Wait...what? What do you mean what is that supposed to mean?"

"You said I know how Seleste is."

"Yeah, that's your girl. Of course you know how Seleste is."

"Well, how did you mean it?"

"Woman, I did not call you to talk about Seleste. I called to talk about you."

"What about me?"

"Oh my gawd. Okay, you're tripping. It sounds like you want to argue and I'm not going for it. Why are you acting so moody? You on your period or something?" Cara didn't answer. There went my stomach again. Flopping and turning. Maybe I needed to eat. My imagination was getting to me. "Or not." Still no answer. I turned the corner on 87th street and turned into a fast food restaurant drive-thru. After looking on the menu, I started my large order to the cashier, and then said, "Man, I'm eating like you."

"What are you trying to insinuate, Jermaine?" Cara snapped.

"You know what? You never did answer that question I asked you about being pregnant."

"Who told you that?"

"Nobody, but you are acting up. I'm starting to think you are."

"Sir, please drive around," the intercom voice said. I whipped my head around to it, suddenly realizing I was having a private conversation with whoever was listening inside of the restaurant.

"Aw my bad," I said and drove up to the first window to pay. Cara didn't respond while I drove from the first window to the second one. I looked down at the clock on my phone and saw the minutes still moving so I knew she hadn't hung up. I pressed the automatic button to lift my windows up and turned on the air conditioning. "Cara, is there something I need to know?"

"What do you want to know?"

I snapped, "What'd I ask you twice already?"

"You don't have to get an attitude with me."

"Oh my gawd. I'm about to hang up this phone. Call me back when you're in a better mood." No answer back. I looked down at my phone and the numbers weren't moving anymore. She'd hung up on me. Enough of the bull. I made a u-turn and headed to Seleste's house. If anybody knew what Cara's problem was, she would.

       *   *   *

When Seleste buzzed me into the inside locked door of her apartment, I yanked the door open and ran up the two flights of stairs, jogging down the hallway to her opened door. Shep jumped on my legs so I'd pet him, but I clumsily stepped over the two and a half foot Labrador Retriever and walked into the kitchen where she was draining something that looked like frozen frying oil. It smelled good in the house but I knew whatever she was cooking was not going to taste that way.

I sat down on one of her barstool chairs in the eating area and turned so I was facing her.

"Jermaine, you're musty. The washroom is that way," she said, pointing towards her bathroom and laughing. I didn't laugh. The smile left her face and she turned to put the mushy, off yellow concoction into a skillet.

"Why did you leave Atlanta early?"

"I told you already."

"No, you actually didn't."

"I was done with what I had to do. I came back to deal with the lease situation with C.C."

Before I could reply, her buzzer went off. She walked to her front door to press the talk button. Memo announced himself, and she buzzed him up. She walked in the kitchen again and broke the stuff in the skillet into small squares.

"You plan on answering my question?"

"What question?" she asked turning one of the dials on her electric stove.

I heard the doorknob turn and Memo came around the corner to the kitchen. "Seleste, for the millionth time, start locking your doors. I hope you didn't leave doors unlocked like this in New York. People get robbed here too." He reached out to hug her and kissed her neck.

"I only left it unlocked because you were coming up," she said, turning to kiss him on the mouth. He slid his hands down to her butt and pulled her closer. "Mr. Romance, look behind you."

Memo looked from her to my grumpy face and released her. "Hey Jermaine, what's going on with you?" He held his hand out and we shook.

"That's what I'm trying to find out," I replied.

Seleste went back to busying herself with what I assumed was food. Memo turned to look at us and then into the skillet. "Oh my gawd, do you have to eat tofu everyday?"

"It's good protein," she answered.

"I know what else would be good. If somebody told me what was going on with Cara, that would help me out a lot. Seleste, why did you leave Atlanta early?" I said.

Memo turned to her. "Yeah, why did you leave early?"

She flipped pieces of the tofu over to brown it and opened cabinets to pull out different seasonings. "Memo, you said you had something to tell me when you got here. What was it?"

Now it was Memo's turn to clam up. I grabbed both the salt and pepper shakers and turned them upside down.

"What are you doing?" Seleste exclaimed, reaching for them. If there was anything Seleste hated more than animal cruelty, it was disorganization. I pressed one hand into her stomach so she couldn't come closer.

"If you don't tell me what's going on, I'm pouring all of this on the floor," I threatened. Shep looked back and forth at us, wagging his tail. Memo walked by us and sat on the living room couch perpendicular to the dining area. She yelled for me to put the shakers down and I started shaking them wildly. She looked to Memo for help, but he'd kicked off his shoes and grabbed the television remote.

"Jermaine. This isn't fair. This is the kind of thing that Cara needs to tell you."

I continued to wave the shakers. Salt and pepper bounced off of the white blinds behind me.

"Stop it," she screamed. Shep barked. I put the containers back on her table. As friendly as Shep was, he'd been trained by Seleste's roommate while Seleste was gone. I didn't know what the mutt would do, but I'd only seen him once since Seleste left. Never know what kind of training class C.C. could've taken Shep to.

"Seleste, if there's something serious going on, you should tell me," I said.

"Something wrong with Cara?" Memo asked, turning around to look at us again.

"She's pregnant," Seleste blurted out. There went my stomach again. I hadn't had the chance to eat the food I bought. It was still in the car.

"Congratulations Jermaine," Memo said with a smile. He looked at Seleste. "That wasn't so bad, now was it?"

I looked at Seleste and as soon as she reached up to twirl a chunk of the back of her hair, I knew there was more to the story. She looked at me looking at her arm and from the look on her face, I could tell that she knew she was caught. "And what else?" I asked.

She looked down at the brown tofu and poured some kind of sweet n' sour sauce on it with rice. The smell of it made me hungry, but this wasn't the time nor the meal I wanted. She turned the dial to let the food simmer and looked back at me still glaring at her. "Jermaine, please don't put me in this position. This is something that Cara has to tell you herself. I can't do it."

"And why not?"

"Because she and I are best friends."

"Last I checked, you and I were too."

Seleste didn't answer that. Slowly, I stood up and got ready to walk to the door, but she blocked me. "Jermaine, you cannot be mad at me. This is just something that I feel Cara should tell you even though we're friends too."

"Whatever. Until I find out what else is going on, you can tell your girl I'm not marrying her." I moved by her, unlocked the door, and yanked it open. The door slammed open so hard that it hit the wall. I stormed down the hall and out of the double doors into my car. Picking up the burger, I ate half of it in one bite and devoured the fries. If I couldn't satisfy my curiosity, I'd at least get rid of the hunger pain.

Chapter 15: Seleste

I closed the door and turned on my heels to confront Memo. "Thanks a lot for helping me," I muttered.

He had one arm across his face and his head lying against the armrest of my couch. "What was I supposed to do? I don't get involved in disputes with family and friends. That never turns out right. Two seconds later, y'all are back to being cool."

"You didn't have to ask me why I came home early. You instigated it."

He moved his arm away from his face, looked up at me standing over him, and cupped his hand around my calf to massage it. "Seleste, if I hadn't've been here, Jermaine would've still had the same questions. Your story doesn't make sense to me though. You left because Cara was pregnant? What's the big deal about her being pregnant?"

I sat down in between the center of his legs and pulled his right leg over my lap. "It's not his baby," I whispered, leaning my head against the back of the couch.

He shot straight up and asked me to repeat myself. I did. "Whose baby is it then?"

I curled my legs under me. "Arnez's."

"Wow. How do you know? Cara told you?"

"Yeah, it happened before Jermaine and her got back together. You know they weren't together when I left for New York so I guess while I was gone, she found out. If she's over three months, Jermaine is going to figure it out anyway. He wasn't messing with her like that during the time that Arnez was."

"Arnez never told us anything about it. Does he know?"

"Yep, and he's happy Jermaine is marrying her, according to Cara. He doesn't want kids and this is his excuse. You know Jermaine would take care of the child like it's his own."

Memo yawned. "Not when he finds out it really isn't his and who it's by."

I shrugged. "Well, I guess that's for him to decide. But if he loves her enough, he might."

"I don't love any woman enough to be taking care of someone else's child, especially if they won't even tell me."

My eyes widened. "So you mean to tell me if you and Cherese were still together and she had..."

He put his hand over my mouth. "Before you even finish that question, don't ask me anything about Cherese. We're not together. We will never be together. And speaking of Cherese, I have to go back to New York this weekend." I reached up to twirl the back of my hair and moved to the other side of the couch, but Memo yanked me back towards him. "Stop doing that. Every time Cherese's name comes up, we end up arguing."

With my arms folded, I asked, "What reason do you have to go back to New York?"

"Terrell is there."

My mouth dropped. "How do you know?"

"Terrell was never the brightest dude on Earth. He tried to hide out at Cherese's house but he kept answering the phone. I called once to see if she knew where he was at, and he answered the phone but I didn't recognize his voice. Jeremiah still calls Cherese all the time to talk because they were so close when she and I were together. So he called there and he answered the phone again hollering about her not coming home. He thought he was talking to her on the phone. Why she'd call her own house instead of just coming back, no idea. Jeremiah called her cell phone, and Cherese is hiding out at her mother's house."

"So where is he now?"

"Still there. He can't go anywhere else because nobody else will let him stay there. Jeremiah asked her to tell my old friends about it so they'd go get him out of her house, but she said she didn't want to do that since she'd be putting my mother's business in the street."

"How come she won't just call the police then?"

Memo shrugged. "Cops are shady. He got out of jail early because of some favors his friends on the police force did for him. I guess she doesn't want to take that chance. She doesn't know who she can trust. If she goes to my boys in my old spot, then they might end up in jail for fighting a cop."

"But he's not a cop anymore."

"Yeah well, some people will never see it that way, mainly the ones in blue."

"Damn. It's hard to get a cop in trouble."

"Exactly. That's why it took years before somebody figured out that Terrell was crooked. Too many other people in his department doing dirt with him. It wasn't until some new guys came on the force that Terrell started getting nervous, mainly the one who chipped my tooth."

I glanced at Memo's tooth when he said that. When I first met him, I asked him what happened to his tooth and he gave me a clipped answer about the chipped tooth being the reason he was in Chicago, but I'd never gotten the story out of him. At the time, I didn't know him well enough to pry. But this time, he told me that he'd tried to sell something to get his father out on bail, but the transaction went wrong when a new cop caught and arrested him. "I only spent the weekend there though. Somebody pulled a few strings and I was out by Monday, but with everything going on with my father, my mother didn't want to risk filing a case against the cop who hit me in the mouth. It would've brought more attention to me and my father, and he would've been in jail longer."

"So what made him go to Cherese's house now?"

"You might not remember this, but that's who he stayed with when he first got out of jail. Cherese was really tight with most of us, minus my mother. My mother never liked her. She thought she was a golddigger."

"Was she?"

Memo nodded. "Yeah, a little bit. But, she was raised like that so it was kind of expected. When I met her, I knew what I was dealing with, but she was cool so..." He paused. "Anyway, that's not the point. The point is that I'm going to New York."

"To confront him?"

"That's one way of looking at it."

I watched his eyes harden and realized that he had no intentions of letting Terrell see the light of day as soon as he set foot in Brooklyn. "Memo, you're about to graduate. Please do not do anything stupid. I know this isn't what you want to hear, but this is something your mother needs to handle. If she's already filed a report on him, she needs to go to the police and tell them that she knows where he's at. You getting involved will make the situation worse."

"Nah, it'll make the situation go away. He tried to kill my mother."

I put my hand on Memo's cheek. "And if you go to jail for killing Terrell, that really will kill her."

Memo opened his mouth to respond, and his cell vibrated. He looked down at the number curiously and then answered. To my surprise, he handed it to me. I never gave out his number or took calls on his phone so I didn't know who it was.

"Hello?"

"You bitch!" Cara screamed into my ear. "You told him. I told you not to tell him and you did. You're jealous. I can't believe you'd do something like that to me."

I squinted my eyes and counted to ten before I responded. "Why are you calling me on Memo's phone?"

Shamontiel L. Vaughn

"You know why I'm calling you on Memo's phone. You turned your ringer off, and you've been avoiding my calls for the past few days. But you took it too far this time. I told you not to tell him, and you did it anyway. When I have this child, you will not be the godmother."

Gripping the phone tighter to my ear, I screamed, "I couldn't give a fuck about being the godmother to your child. Don't blame me for a situation you should've handled on your own. You should never have said you were going to marry Jermaine and not tell him Arnez was the father. That's really messed up. Don't blame me because you can't keep your legs closed."

"Aw, so you think you're perfect now because you only got one man to open your legs up to? Well, look here, sweetheart, don't try to act like I was cocking my legs open to everybody. I was with Arnez all by myself and Jermaine all by myself, never together. Don't try to act like I'm some type of ho. But regardless of what I do, that gave you no right to tell him."

"He came to my house demanding that I tell him something. I didn't give him any reason to look at you. He had to get his suspensions from someone else. I'm going to give you a little advice though. If you really want to keep a secret, don't tell anybody. I don't know why you expected me to keep that to myself. Jermaine was my friend long before you, and I would never want to keep something like that away from him."

"Did you have to tell him that it was Arnez's baby?"

"I didn't tell him that."

I waited for her rebuttal, but instead I heard crying. "Hello?"

"You didn't tell him that?"

"No. I just told him you were pregnant."

More crying. "I thought you told him. When he called me yelling about the wedding being off, I told him Arnez meant nothing to me and..."

114

I listened to her cry some more, but I wasn't about to comfort her, especially after she'd called me out of my name and accused me of something I didn't do.

"What am I supposed to do?" she said through hiccups.

I didn't know how to answer her. The whole situation was frustrating to me. Arnez not owning up to his child and being willing to give Jermaine all of the responsibility. Cara trying to trick Jermaine into being with her regardless of her circumstances. Jermaine calling off the wedding. Memo going to New York to confront Terrell. Renee almost being raped and scared to be in her own home so much that Memo was there to make her feel safe. Jeremiah having to deal with all of this news that Cherese told him, even though she should have picked up the phone to call Memo instead. Cara and I possibly not being friends anymore. Worst of all, Terrell putting Cherese back into the picture.

Chapter 16: Arnez

Grabbing the woman's head up, I yelled, "You're putting your teeth on it! What is wrong with you?"

She wiped her mouth and looked at me with pleading eyes. "I've never done this before."

I sighed and laid back against the bed. "Just leave. You don't know what you're doing. Just get out. I don't have time to teach anybody how to handle business."

She held the tip of it and instead of leaving, she tried again. I watched her head go up and down, and up and down until I couldn't even see it anymore. What a liar. Talking about she never gave head before. I told her she had to leave and now she's miraculously a professional. My stomach started churning and I closed my eyes, hoping the nausea would stop. I'd been getting sick regularly now and blamed it on the changing of the weather. Chicago was weird like that, cold one day and hot the next. But being sick in the middle of May sucked. I was trying to make the most of it, but this chick trying to suck me off was not helping at all. The more she did it, the more I wanted to throw up. I pulled her microbraids away from my body, and she sat up with a sly smile on her face. I guess the dummy thought she was working me over because she turned so her butt was facing me, ready for entrance. I coughed and felt the bile in my throat. This cold I had was becoming agonizing. I'd never been this sick before, and I was in pretty good shape. Maybe I had pneumonia. I stood up slowly, and she grabbed the back of me to pull in closer to her, but instead I moved away and jogged to the suite bathroom. Jogging with a hard-on is no easy task, but it was either that or unload all over the bed, and that definitely would've been a turn-off. I ran water over my face and spit a few times into the toilet. Grabbing a washcloth to rub my face, I noticed a couple of purple bumps close to my eyelids. They weren't quite pimples, just strange marks. Maybe I was breaking out. Even though I'd lost about 10 pounds in the past month, I'd been eating more greasy food than usual since football season was over. I still tried to lift weights regularly and run, but that was to keep in shape, not to lose any weight. My coach always made the team members get regular check-ups and as much as I hated going to doctors, I guess I'd have to now.

I gargled and stood up, still erect. When I headed back into my dorm room, I turned to lock the door so my suitemates wouldn't barge in, and looked at the woman. I wish I could remember her name before I started telling her all of the stuff I wanted to do to her. She looked at me through slit eyes and slowly cocked her legs open. I ran back into the bathroom once again. I heard her knocking at the door asking me if I was okay. I laid on the side of the cold, tile floor and closed my eyes. My feet had been burning a little. I remember when my grandmother had problems with her feet, she had gout. I rubbed my forehead and laid my head against the wall. I didn't want her to see me like this, but I had to find a way to get her out without looking like a chump. I stood up again slowly and reached for a pair of my boxers hanging on the hook by the shower. When they were securely around my waist, I opened the door again.

"Arnez, what's wrong?"

"I need you to leave."

"Why?"

"Just get out. I don't want to talk about it."

I saw the hurt look on her beige face and in those mahogany brown eyes. Her eyelashes were so curly to the point that I was convinced they were fake. Her body was chiseled a little bit like Cherese's. My cheeks puffed out at the thought of Cherese. She'd called me a month ago, accusing me of giving her some disease. Anita had too.

When Jermaine asked me about it, I didn't want to hear more stories from those liars. Even when this girl asked me to use a condom, I ignored her and went in bare. I didn't even own condoms anymore. I didn't want to live my life worried about anything but sex and lots of it. But before I could do that, I needed to go to the drug store to get some cold medicine. I waited for her to get dressed and jerked my head away when she tried to kiss me goodbye. None of the niceties. I just wanted her gone. I sat on the end of my bed and lost my breath. A pain shot through my side, and I laid on it. I wondered what kind of pneumonia this could be.

*   *   *

I went to the university physician for a physical and after she'd made me do every known imaginable thing to embarrass a man, she recommended that I get a blood test to find out what was going wrong with my system. I called the doctor's office that she recommended me to and they were closed for the weekend. I drove straight to the emergency room. I didn't have two days to spare and another girl was coming over that same night. After pricking what felt like a hundred needles in me for various tests, a doctor came into the examination room.

She sat down in front of me and asked me about my cold symptoms. I told her everything that had been happening to me over the past couple of months, and as she slowly nodded her head, I got the impression that there was something she wasn't telling me. She smiled a fake smile and said she'd call me as soon as the results came in, but she asked me to take it easy and get plenty of sleep.

I climbed slowly into my truck and sat there. My vision was a little fuzzy. I brainstormed on who I could call to tail me and make sure I didn't crash into anybody. For the past week, I'd gotten Jermaine's voicemail every time I called. Memo was in New York dealing with the situation with his father. Seleste didn't really like me much so I knew she wouldn't want to come. I'd been avoiding Cara all semester ever since she told me she was pregnant so she definitely wasn't getting a call. I smiled when I realized the one person who I knew would have my back and dialed his number.

"Yeah, what's up?" O greeted me.

"Hey, man, I'm at the emergency room."

"What happened?

"I don't know. I think I got some kind of cold or something. Been feeling kind of bad lately. You think you could come pick me up?"

"Aw man, I'm sorry. My car died on me again. You're going to have to call a cab."

"That's too expensive. Forget it. I'll just drive."

"Did you try Memo and Jermaine already?"

I leaned my head against the steering wheel and blinked a few times. "Nah, I'm good. I'm good. I'll be all right."

"You sure?"

"Yeah man, I'm good."

I got off the phone with him and started my SUV up. Turning out of the parking lot on Western, I cut a right on 95th street and rode straight until I got to the entrance of I-94. Merging into expressway traffic, I turned the music up loud when I heard my favorite song on the radio. Reciting the lyrics to the song, I started speeding up, dipping in and out between slow cars. I looked in my rearview mirror to see a car behind me doing the same thing. Can't even blame him. Some people shouldn't even have a license. A prime example was the truck in front of me going slower than my grandmother drove. I tried to cut a right but the truck edged to its left in my lane, pushing me into the passing lane where people were headed to the express lane. Swerving around the truck, I gave him the finger and went in front of him, but the car that was speeding around like me was trying to take the same spot. I braked quickly so I wouldn't hit the side of my car against the other car, but the truck didn't brake. Before I knew it, my truck was flipping upside down, and I smelled gas before I blacked out.

Part 2

Part 2

Chapter 17: Cara

I'd planned to come back to Chicago the week after Jermaine and I got into the argument, but the news about Arnez brought me back quicker. I was sitting on my grandfather's porch swing when I got the call. When I answered, O told me that Arnez had been in a truck accident. A day later, I sat in the airport reading a magazine and trying to figure out how to handle both situations. Before I could board the plane, I got another call from O. I looked at my watch estimating how long it would take me to get to whatever hospital he was at once my plane landed. O kept talking. There would be no hospital visits. O said that although Arnez went into the hospital for a truck accident, Arnez didn't survive. He didn't die because of the accident though. He died due to complications with AIDS. His body couldn't fight the injuries because he'd been too far along, lost too much blood, and apparently was already sick.

I sat in the airport stunned. If Arnez had AIDS, that meant the potential for our baby was even more likely. Disconnecting the call with O about funeral arrangements, I looked down at the magazine. It was open to an ad about expecting mothers, but where was the page about how to deal with a baby who could suffer for life?

*   *   *

The airplane landed two and a half hours later and I headed to the bagging area pondering on who I could call to pick me up. Jermaine was avoiding my calls, Seleste had changed her phone number altogether, and I knew O would want to talk about Arnez again so that was out. I wasn't ready to come to the realization that my child wouldn't have a father. Memo had enough on his mind and I didn't want to bother him, so I called my brother.

*   *   *

After I'd dropped my things off, my brother took me directly to the hospital. I'd told him the news and he went into father mode. Typical. All the time I'd stayed with my brother, he always had my back. When I went back to Atlanta, my grandfather was like a father. My real father was unknown and my mother was still street hopping. If my grandmother was still alive, I could've called her for comfort. I needed a female voice to tell me everything was okay. I looked down at my phone and thought about calling Memo to reach Seleste. But if she changed her number, I knew she didn't want to be bothered. So, I held my brother's hand in the emergency room and hoped for the best.

*   *   *

After I left the hospital, with my gynecologist telling me everything looked all right, my brother took me to my dorm. I'd paid a little extra to have no roommate and today, I was glad I did. I laid onto my back with my head against a pillow. I was getting ready to doze off when something blue caught my attention. I looked over at my desk and saw a blue tie lying on the desk chair. Standing up, I glanced at a note safety pinned to it from Jermaine asking me was that color okay. During the winter semester, I'd moved out of the women's dormitory to a co-ed one, and since then, Jermaine could come and go as he pleased. He had the other key, although he lived in his frat house, but spent most of his time here with me. When I wasn't here, I'd find random cards and a couple of times, I found flowers. Seeing a reminder of him brought a smile to my face. I sat down in my desk chair and smelled the tie, which smelled like his cologne. I looked in the make-up mirror on my desk and tied the fabric around my neck. I'd seen him wear the tie a couple of times: once on his way to church and another time the day he won an award for his success with our college radio station. Holding the tip of the tie in my hand, tears fell onto silk, turning blue to navy.

*   *   *

Six hours later, I woke up to a dark room. My alarm clock said it was 10:38 pm. This was around the time that I'd usually call Seleste on weekends to go to whatever party Jermaine's fraternity was throwing or whatever else was happening on campus. Some students went home for the weekend, so it would usually be the same crews hanging out.

I pulled up my shirt and my stomach was flat as usual, even though my cheeks were slightly chubby. My chest probably wouldn't grow any larger, considering it was already huge. I walked to my full-length mirror and looked at myself. I'd put sew-in braids in my head. It hurt a little, but I wasn't supposed to be using chemicals on my hair so I dealt with it the same way I was dealing with everything else. If this was what motherhood was going to be like, I didn't want any part of it. I liked clubs and laying on my stomach too much to deal with five more months of this. I wondered if Jermaine would've liked my braids. I know Arnez would have. He use to play in my hair all the time when we'd watch movies. He and I didn't go on dates, but we did hang out.

I use to like watching him play football during the games and laugh at him showboating at step competitions. I wondered how the rest of his frat was taking the bad news. I didn't feel like it was real. Even though he could be a jerk sometimes, I was still convinced he looked out for me. Hell, I was the one who never wanted to use condoms. Pills were enough, so I thought.

When I told him I was pregnant, we'd been sitting on the stairs on the other side of our library. He'd stared at the grass for a long time and leaned his muscular build back against the step above his elbows.

"So what do you want to do?" he asked.

I'd shrugged. "It just seems awkward. You know Jermaine and I are trying to work things out, and you don't really want to commit."

"I'm not really ready to settle down or be anybody's father."

"I'm not ready to be anybody's mother but you know I've always been ready to settle down."

"If you tell Jermaine, I think he'll break up with you."

"I know he will, but it's not fair to keep it a secret either. He asked me to marry him." I looked into Arnez's eyes to see if there was any hint of jealousy but his expression showed shock.

"Whoa, Beatz really loves you. I knew that though. When you use to play those games with me about going to his dorm room when you'd get mad at me, I knew eventually he was going to wear you down." He reached his hand up and scratched the back of his head. Leaning forward, he placed both of his arms on his knees and placed his face in his palms. "Cara, that's the man you need to be with. All I want to do is play football and party. He's ready to give you the life you want."

"So you don't want any part in this baby's life at all?" I leaned forward to look into his eyes.

He turned his head so he was facing me. "Cara, why did you get pregnant?"

My eyes tightened. "What do you mean why? I'm not trying to trap you."

"You never wanted to use anything. Claimed the pills worked. I don't get it."

"Nothing is 100%. And you knew it just like I did so don't try to place the blame."

"I'm not blaming anybody. I'm just saying I don't want to be involved. Might sound harsh, but it's the truth. You can change your mind about having that kid any time you want to. I can't. I don't want to be stuck with something I don't want."

I stood up shaking my head. "Same ole Arnez. Selfish as hell. You know what? How about you do me a favor and never talk to me again?"

He stood up and, even though his 5'9 frame towered over my 5'1 frame, I stood strong and dared him to do something stupid. But instead, he leaned over, kissing me on the forehead. "I ain't the man for you. Jermaine is. I just did you a favor by telling you that." Then he walked away. That was the last time I had a face-to-face conversation with him, and now I'd never have that opportunity again. Life is too short. I picked up the phone and dialed.

Chapter 18: Memo

"Why do they need you to come identify him? It's not like they didn't know who he was already," I said.

"Who are you telling? Honestly I just want to make this trip and leave," my mother said. I looked over at her. She'd lost a little weight, and slightly purple half moons curled under her eyes. Still wearing sweaters but moved from pants to capris. It barely got scorching hot in Brooklyn anyway. There were nice days, but it was like being in Chicago. It felt like déjà vu sitting in yet another police station waiting to talk to someone. I'd called Cherese three times at her mother's house, but she kept saying she wasn't there. I had questions to ask her about this letter that Terrell had mailed to me. Some things on the notebook paper he scribbled on were things I'd never want to share with my mother, but I sure as hell would've appreciated Cherese sharing with me.

I walked with my mother into a room that had double mirrors so we could see into them but the people we observed couldn't see us. The identification process was pointless because both Terrell and I knew who was on each side, but my mother wrapped the sweater tighter around her body when he looked straight ahead. I stared at his bushy eyebrows and messed-up hairline, all the way down to his dirty t-shirt and rugged gym shoes. He looked homeless and like he smelled bad, but I'd know him a mile away.

When we stepped off the plane, my mother asked me what I would do if she didn't identify him in a line-up. She said as long as he stayed away from her, she didn't care what he did in another state. Her concern was that he'd get out early again. I told her if she didn't make him go to jail for what he did, I would end up in jail for murdering him. She pulled her suitcase faster, and we hopped into a cab.

She pointed him out to the officer and after a few more questions and paperwork, we went back outside to look for a cab. She whistled to one driving by and when it stopped, she scrambled to get in before someone else took it from her. When I didn't join her inside, she leaned out of the car curiously. I told her I had to make a pit stop, and she demanded that I didn't miss my flight. Nodding my head, I walked the opposite way and headed towards one of the subway stations. Humid and crowded as hell. Storming off the train at my stop, I pushed past other riders and up the stairs to the street.

I walked several blocks to Cherese's mother's house and saw some familiar faces. A couple guys looked out for the police while one of my old friends leaned over in a car. Before I could walk completely by them, Dos yelled out to me.

"¿Que paso? Fuck you doing over here?" Dos greeted me, standing up straight as the car drove on. Dos was a Dominican cat, known for being one of the friendliest but most dangerous guys in Brooklyn. Hiking boots clean enough to be new, a baggy jean outfit with a name brand stamped all over the place on it, and a mass of curls wilder than mine all over his head. I use to tease him all the time about his color contacts. One day, his eyes would be hazel, then gray, and devil red with claws where the pupils should've been. Normally I'd be happy to see him, but that day I wasn't trying to kick it. I gave him a pound and half hug, then looked up to the second floor of the building we stood in front of.

"Oh, I see. Came to get Cherese back, huh?" He laughed. "You're too late for that, son. They moved."

I turned to look at him. "What? Every time I call, I get an answering machine."

He rolled his presently green eyes. "It's 2007, kid. What? When people move in Chi-town, they don't let you keep the same number?"

"Aw, you got jokes. Where did she move to?"

He shook his head and turned to see another car pull up. "Hold on for a second." Walking over to a new car, he talked a couple minutes, exchanged products, and walked back my way.

"You're still doing that? I thought you and your breaking crew were going to tour."

"We are. But it doesn't pay the bills like this does. Everybody doesn't have a mother to put him through college."

I got ready to point out that my mother hadn't paid a dime for me to go to school. My football scholarship got me through my freshman and sophomore year and most of my junior year before I was kicked off the team for fighting the coach. Loans paid the rest of the way until I got the job with the parole officer, right next to the station my mother had gone to report Terrell to. The same station where I could possibly get paperwork on witnesses and see why Cherese moved.

"What you grinning for?" Dos asked me.

I didn't even realize I was smiling while I was plotting. "It's been good seeing you, Dos."

He looked a little confused as he tapped my fist. I quickly started walking and he yelled out, "Where are you going? You going to the Bronx to find her?"

"The Bronx is where she's at now?"

He nodded. "You going? I'll go with you. Me and some of the crew are going to this new club in Manhattan tonight. You should come with us after that."

I knew if I stayed there through the night, I'd end up drunk and with nothing accomplished. "Nah, I'm going to pass. Been good seeing you, man." I turned to walk away.

"Running back to Chicago, huh? I should come visit you. Must be something for you to leave Brooklyn for good."

I stopped and turned around. "I'm always going to be Brooklyn for life, but you know, I got love for Chicago. Thanks for telling me about Cherese though."

Dos got ready to say something else but another car rolled up and he was back to business. He threw up the peace sign at me and turned to walk to the car. By the time I got to the airport, I was relieved that there were the electronic check-in machines because I would've missed my flight standing in the long lines. I sat next to my mother, who was dozing off in and out. She looked too drained to ask me where I'd been, so she just yawned and laid her head on my shoulder. That made me think of Seleste. I told her I'd call her as soon as I came back. Before I left, she had this strange look on her face. I knew she had her suspicions about why I needed to see Cherese, but she didn't know about the letter. I don't know what made Terrell send me this, but he must've known he was going back to jail. I pulled the letter from my back pocket and read it for the hundredth time since I'd gotten it a few days ago.

May 9, 2007

To Travis:

I know you don't want to hear from me, but I feel like I have a right to tell my side of the story. This isn't going to be one of these letters saying I didn't do the crime, just telling you what was on my mind. Your mother is a wonderful woman, and I tried to do my best by her but being an officer is hard. You try to keep the bad guys off the street, but there are so many bad guys that want you off the street to the point where you become one. When I got out of prison, I shouldn't have automatically gone back to your mother. I should've gotten my mind right on my own instead of messing with somebody else's.

When you get married, you'll learn that there is a certain amount of love and affection that a husband needs from his wife. Considering the circumstances that I came back to, for my own wife to ask me to get tested for STDs, like we were dating, I took that as an insult. Jeremiah isn't even my real son, and even though she cheated back in the day, I never asked her to take a test. But that's neither here nor there because I took that boy in. I will admit that I have played favorites between you two, but I still took him in and forgave her for doing what she did. But somehow, she couldn't forgive me for my indiscretions. And even when I did get tested, I didn't know I had it. And for the record, I was never raped in prison. Ever.

When the doctors told me that we could still have a sexual relationship but with contraception, your mother freaked out. She wanted to know how I got it. The prison rape story was the easiest way I could get her to trust me again. So that's what I told her. She was still too scared to do anything. Now I won't give you all the details because you are my son and I know that might be uncomfortable for you, but I got ahold of everything under the sun to get her to change her mind.

She started using excuses about cramps, Jeremiah being home, and headaches. Finally, I got fed up with it. Imagine not doing anything with the woman you married for almost four years without her touching you. And then she gives you excuses. Well, I'm sure she already told you what happened next, but what she may not have told you was that I did try to use protection. No matter what I did, I would never pass on anything to kill my wife.

You may be wondering why I came back to New York. I wanted to confront the person who could've given me the disease. You see the return address label. I took it from her desk so you already know where I'm at. Cherese loved you so much and still does. I always liked her and wanted you to marry her.

But for whatever reason, you dumped her. When I came to stay with her after I was released, I didn't think I'd ever see your mother again. Hell, she skipped states to get away from me and we'd been married for over ten years. Can you blame me for thinking she was gone for good? I thought I'd start my life over with a new woman.

Every time I read that part, I always had to stop, breathe, and get a drink of water. I wandered to a restaurant stand and bought a bottled water. Start my life over with a new woman? Never mind who the woman was to his son. Breathing I sat down next to my sleeping mother and continued to read.

You and I both know that I've always thought highly of Cherese, but I respected my wife and your relationship. That's why it wasn't that many times that we did what we did. I can't apologize enough for doing something like that to you, but I can't change the past.

Then your mother came to New York to get me to sign divorce papers. I knew it was wrong to be with Cherese, and I still loved your mother so I came to Chicago. But karma must've caught up with me because I ended up getting something from her. I made her get tested when I came back to confront her. So, I guess I got what I deserved. That's why I didn't run when the cops came. One of them use to be a very good friend of mine. He asked me to run and not come back to New York. But I did enough sneaking the first time on the police force and the second time with Cherese.

Anyway, I just wanted to apologize. I'm sorry for what I did to your mother. I'm sorry about Cherese. I'm sorry about not being a good father to you and Jeremiah. Hopefully you'll be a better father and husband with that new woman you're always grinning about. I'm not supposed to be telling you all of this in the letter, but hell, if the cops skim my mail and you don't receive this, who gives a damn? I'm going to die anyway. I'm more concerned that you forgive me. I love you.

Sincerely,
Your father Terrell

The first time I read this letter, I wrote a two words on the inside flap of the envelope, sealed, and addressed it. I never mailed it though. Instead, I tried to do the right thing and support my mother. Terrell had written her a letter as well, saying he was going to turn himself in. He lied because when we got to the station, we were informed that Cherese's mother was the person who called. Regardless of what my father said, there are two sides of a story. I wanted to hear Cherese's. I looked over at my mother and wondered if her letter admitted who gave him the disease. I wondered if her letter was a reminder that Terrell did use protection and that's why she didn't end up with anything. I wondered why she didn't know he did, but in that situation, I could easily see her not thinking clearly.

I wrapped my arms around my mother and felt guilty that I wasn't there to protect her. When she was asleep, she looked peaceful. But when she woke up, she looked scared and worried. It was hard to see her look so defeated.

I dialed Cherese's mother's number one more time and for the first time, left a voicemail message. "I was there. I need to talk to Cherese about what she did with my father. Hit me back." If her mother didn't know before, she'd know once she heard the message, unless Cherese got to it first.

Chapter 19: Jermaine

I sat on the steps by the bridge and listened to the water from the school fountain. I'd been sitting on the steps for about a half n' hour trying to decide whether I wanted to leave or not. Cara had called me to talk. I didn't have anything to talk about. Earlier that day, we'd gone to Arnez's funeral. His sister, Corleen, was there, along with a bunch of our frat and almost all of the school football team. I saw a gang of women he dated in school. It was hard to fathom someone so close to you disappearing so fast. Initially, everyone believed he died from a truck accident alone, but when speakers were called to the front to speak about him, that's when the mayhem started.

It started off pleasantly with the football players complimenting his skill or making jokes about how brutal he was on the field. Some of the bruhs came up to speak about how hardheaded he was and how they knew he'd cross because of stubbornness. His sister, Corleen, came up to talk about how much she loved him and how protective he was. I watched Cara shift in her seat when his sister asked if there were anymore speakers. Finally she stood up, only to sit back down when Anita beat her to the front. I held my breath and hoped she didn't say anything cruel, but in the back of my mind, I wanted her to. Regardless of how promiscuous Anita was, she didn't deserve not knowing the situation he'd put her in.

She walked up to the front in an evergreen knee-length dress with a wide gold belt, gold hoop earrings, and gold heels on. Still flawlessly fit and gorgeous. I knew she'd be that way until her last days. She cleared her throat and looked around at the audience.

"I won't be up here long but I did want to say a few words. Most of you all know me from around Lace." A couple of snickers were heard. "And some of you don't.

But even if you know of me, you may not know everything. Everything about me or everything about Arnez. But I'll tell you what I do know. Arnez was a complex man. Sometimes he was very nice and looked out for people, like one time when he wouldn't bring me around while he was pledging. He was worried about me acting up. And then other times he wasn't so nice."

Corleen was sitting in the front row when Anita said this, and she turned to whisper to someone sitting next to her. When the woman turned to look at Corleen, I noticed the striking resemblance they had. All of Arnez's family was mainly in Atlanta, where he grew up, so I'd never met anyone besides friends from school.

"I'm not here to start any drama but I see a lot of women holding tissue and sniffing." The woman who resembled Corleen started hissing in Corleen's ear. Anita kept talking and ignored the commotion. "I was crying just like all of you were a few months ago. But I was crying because I couldn't understand why this man..." She pointed at the coffin. "Why he didn't tell me he had AIDS." A hush fell over the crowd and both Corleen and that woman next to her jerked their heads to attention. "While you all are crying about him being in a coffin, I want to cry thinking about how I'll eventually end up in one too." Corleen stood up and whispered something in Anita's ear. "I was told just now not to say anything about this situation, but I feel like you all need to know. Every woman out there who thinks she's immune to it, you better wake up."

"Get that lying bitch out of here," Sweet, one of the bruhs, yelled. "How are you going to put somebody on blast at their funeral?" I looked from Sweet to Anita to Corleen, who was now yanking at Anita's arm to leave. Anita was letting Corleen lead her too, which was surprising considering Anita's arms were solid enough to take Corleen down to the floor if it got violent. Peter, another frat member, held Sweet back as Corleen led Anita out of the funeral home.

The woman who was arguing with Corleen stood up and turned to Sweet. "Young man, I don't care what kind of brother you think you are to Arnez. I'm still his mother, you're not my son, and you will not use that language at his funeral. Keep the foolishness outside." Her eyes started to well up with tears.

Cara did stand up this time and headed to the woman, but another woman's voice yelled out from the back. "It's true. He had it."

Arnez's mother pressed her lips together. "I won't comment on that. I'm not here to talk about Arnez's flaws."

The yelling woman stood up. I turned to see that it was Anita's friend, Lisa, the one who was kicked out of school for fighting Seleste. I looked around for Seleste but she was nowhere in sight. I hadn't talked to her since the day I left her apartment, but she'd left messages apologizing to me on my voicemail. Between her and Cara, my voicemail was full. I looked in Memo's direction, sitting next to O a couple of rows ahead of me, and they both looked surprised. I wondered if I was the only one who knew about Arnez before the funeral.

Lisa yelled, "Lady, a flaw is someone who's moody. A flaw is not someone who gave my best friend his filthy disease."

Corleen came back in at that moment with the funeral director, who escorted Lisa out. I looked back to Cara, who was holding her stomach. Seleste sat down next to her. They both reached out to hug each other, and I felt a lump in my throat. The funeral ended with his mother speaking.

"Now I know everyone has strong opinions about Arnez. He was a strong person with a strong personality, and that's why I love him. I'm not asking everybody here to love him like I do because you never could. But I am going to ask that you don't hold hate in your heart for him. I'd never known my son to be scared of anything. He called me when he was pledging, but told me his friend, Jermaine, helped him through it." A few people glanced my way. "His friends, O and Travis, were his help on the football team." I looked at O and Memo, who were half grinning. "Now I knew O and Memo but I'd never met Jermaine." She looked directly at me. "Nice to see the face behind photos he's shown me." I nodded at her. "A mother always wants to be in her son's life. Keep up with what he's doing and who he's hanging out with. But it's a hard pill to swallow when someone has to deal with something that doesn't end. A football tackle ends. Pledging ends. Even a truck accident doesn't go on forever. But what my son had would never go away. I'd never seen him scared. He admitted that he was scared to me. He told me he was going to keep going, like it hadn't happened. Now, he didn't go about doing it the right way, if what those two young ladies said is correct, but he was a scared young man who knew eventually he was going to..." Her speech broke off into sobs.

Corleen embraced her mother and they walked back to their seats. Some guy I didn't know made a few closing remarks and slowly we all left. I headed to my car to follow everybody to the burial ground when I felt a tap on my shoulder. I turned to see Seleste.

"I...I just....I want to say I'm sorry for not telling you," she started.

I cut her off by hugging her. Some of that hug was to let her know we were still friends, some because a friend of mine had died, but most was out of fear that Cara and her child were going to die. I looked over my shoulder and saw Cara a few feet away, holding one of her elbows with her palm and looking uncomfortable. I turned my head and buried my face in Seleste's neck. I wasn't ready to confront Cara. When Seleste pulled away, she whispered to me,

"Cara wants to talk to you. If you're willing to talk to her, meet her on the library steps tonight around 7 pm."

"I'll think about it," I mumbled. I let her go and watched her and Cara walk to Seleste's car.

"Leave it up to Lisa and Anita to start some shit at a funeral," Memo's voice said behind me. I turned to see him and O standing together. We gave each other pounds and agreed we'd ride in my car instead of taking two separate ones. O told me about Arnez asking him for a ride home and how he felt it was his fault that his car wasn't working properly. I looked through my rearview mirror at O and it suddenly hit me that O would take this the hardest. He was the last one to speak to Arnez and the one who got Arnez to move from Atlanta to Chicago. Those two were friends since freshman year. Memo and I didn't meet Arnez until our junior year. I felt bad. I should've called them to see how they were holding up.

When we got to the burial site, I talked to the bruhs for a few minutes and found out that Anita had done some things with Peter and Sweet. That would explain why they were so mad at Anita's announcement. Those two hadn't shown up nor were the ladies that started the commotion present. After a few words and tears, I dropped O and Memo back off at Memo's car and Seleste took Cara home. Cara kept her distance from me there too. It made me wonder whether the meeting by the stairs was Seleste's idea instead of Cara's.

"I didn't think Seleste could convince you to come," Cara said. I turned around to see her standing on the top step. My reflex was to help her down the stairs, but I was still too surprised that she looked the same to do so. No weight gain besides chubby cheeks. Hair in a new braid style. She wore a lilac and white summer dress and sandals. She looked more like she was headed to the lakefront than to sit on some stairs. She walked down one step and I jumped up. If she fell down those stairs, I'd

140

never forgive myself. I touched her arm and waist, and a hint of a smile crossed her face.

"Thank you," she said, sitting down.

"How you doing?" I asked.

She nodded her head. "I'm good. Morning sickness and all, but you know, I'm good." I watched her lips while she talked and wondered if I'd ever get to kiss them again. She turned her body to me and reached for my hands. I held hers in return. "Jermaine, first I want to apologize for not telling you about me being pregnant. I was going to get another abortion, but the doctors told me if I did, I'd probably never be able to have kids again." I nodded, remembering her telling me about a past boyfriend who she'd had an abortion for. "I just didn't know how to tell you. I was shocked when I found out because I hadn't messed with Arnez since the days I caught him with Anita. I wasn't showing and my cycle is moody, so I didn't think I was pregnant. But one day, I started getting nauseous in the morning and I went to the school nurse to see if I had pneumonia or something."

"Do you? Do you have… anything?"

She shook her head no. "The doctor said I was pregnant then and nothing else. I went to another doctor while I was in Georgia, and she said the same thing. I was irresponsible with Arnez, but I didn't get it. I don't even understand how Anita got it since I didn't, unless Anita gave it to him."

"Or someone else. Anita saw me at the lakefront and said he gave it to her."

She shrugged. "Well, it wasn't like Arnez was faithful to me or anyone else so it could've been anybody. But not me."

I was relieved. Regardless of her not being pregnant by me, I didn't want her to lose her child. "So you didn't cheat on me?"

Her eyes widened. "No! Why would I do that? I love you to death."

She caught a brotha in the heart with that one. "I wish you would've told me when you found out though. I keep wondering what would have happened if Seleste hadn't broken down. Would you really have let me marry you knowing that?"

She gripped my hands tighter. "You and I both know that Seleste is the worst liar ever. Once I told her, I knew she'd tell you whether I wanted her to or not. So subconsciously, I wanted you to know."

I moved my hands away from her. "Cara, marriage doesn't survive off of subconscious thoughts. You're either honest or you're not."

"That's very true. All I can do is apologize for that. Even if we can just be friends, I'd hope you could accept my apology one of these days."

I leaned back and put my head on the step above. "This whole situation is crazy. I don't even know who to trust. Arnez could be responsible for other people and lied to my face about Anita. You're pregnant and didn't tell me. Seleste tried to keep it from me. Right now, the only people in my corner are the bruhs and Memo." The expression on Cara's face was hurt. "Cara, I appreciated the apology, but right now I need time. I've already canceled the reservations and my suit."

Her eyes filled with tears. "I canceled everything too. I knew you'd say that."

"Yeah. You do know me well. But you should've known being pregnant was something you should've told me, especially from Arnez. Did he know?"

Tears started flying down her face. Her not answering was a good enough answer for me. "I don't believe he knew that he had that disease…or he didn't have it when he was with me…but I did tell him about…her."

My eyebrows raised. A little Cara. She'd be beautiful. I hoped she didn't look like Arnez. Actually I hoped this was all a book, and I could die in this chapter. Or a bad dream. I pinched myself and looked around for something unrealistic. To my disappointment, this was as real as I thought.

"Cara, I really just don't know what to say to you. I don't know if I want to be with you anymore. I don't know if I want to be friends with you. I do know that I got to get out of here though." I stood up. She didn't. "Do you want a ride back to the dorm?"

She shook her head no, but reached her hand up. I thought she wanted help up the stairs, but when she only touched my palm, I felt a warm new weight. She put her hands on her knees and turned away from me. I walked up the steps and didn't look in my hand until I got to my car in the dorm lot. I opened the door and sat down, turned my CD player to a slow jam mixtape I'd made, and twirled the engagement ring in my hand. I watched students walking by pulling suitcases, getting ready for summer break. Cara usually took summer classes like me and I stayed on campus. I didn't even know if she'd be on campus or going back to Georgia for the summer.

I people-watched for a couple of hours and finally got out of the car to walk across the parking lot to the frat house.

Chapter 20: Cherese

"Are you ever going to call him back?" my mother, Golden, asked me daily for the first few days I camped out at her place.

I'd shrug and say, "What am I supposed to say? Sorry your parents didn't work out."

With a cigarette in her hand, she'd blow out smoke and respond, "You could start off like that."

A week ago, I'd moved to the Bronx with her when Terrell took over my place, once he and I reached an agreement. If I let him hide at my place, then he wouldn't tell Memo about our situation or my physical condition. The problem was that neither of us considered my mother having an issue with him. I told her he subleased the apartment. She didn't buy it. She called the police to check my story and found out that NYPD was looking for him too. He was arrested on the spot.

The police made me come to the station and explain why he was staying at my apartment. I stuck to my story about Terrell needing a place after he told me that he and his wife split up again. The detective looked at me and nodded. Then he handed me a bunch of my mail and one opened letter with the word, copy, stamped on it. He told me to read the letter and as I did, my nervous energy turned into exasperation.

When I looked up at the detective, he was reading me my rights. I spent the rest of the day in jail until my mother's boyfriend and my mother bailed me out. On my way out, one of the detectives instructed me not to go too far.

The next morning, I went back to my old place to retrieve the rest of my stuff, and my landlord told me I had to go. I hadn't paid rent and with the way the cops came in and tore up my place trying to get to Terrell, they didn't want that type of reputation in their neighborhood. I scowled and put a hood over my head when I saw a bunch of journalists outside of my place. I power walked to Golden's boyfriend's car with the rest of my things in suitcases and zipped my sweatshirt up to my neck. When I got to Golden's place, I took a shower and slept on her couch in her studio apartment. How me, Golden, and her boyfriend, Rod, were supposed to live peacefully when my chances of going to jail was so high, I had no idea. Golden started to spend more time at Rod's house because she was tired of Memo calling, especially when the news stories started to run.

As the weeks rolled by, ridiculous rumors about Terrell and I eloping after he left his wife surfaced. For the millionth time, I wondered why Terrell thought hiding at my apartment would prevent him from getting caught. He thought he was getting revenge in the letter he wrote to me, but he'd screwed himself in the process. I changed the channel to a music station to get my mind off of Terrell, but I kept seeing those stupid wrap-it-up commercials, so I turned the television off altogether. The phone rang repeatedly, but I wasn't just avoiding Memo now. I was avoiding overzealous reporters. I'd gotten an email from the law firm that I completed my internship with, stating that because of my legal issues, they didn't want to hire me for a permanent position.

If Terrell wouldn't have come back to New York, none of this would have happened. After I left the testing center a few weeks ago, I made a call to this guy I grew up with named Dos. Dos was a breaker and a hustler who lived around my old neighborhood. Money was exchanged for a personal visit to Chicago to see Arnez. But I specifically said whoever was sent to just rough Arnez up so he wouldn't do what he did to me to any other women. I got word back that whoever Dos sent to follow him to his dorm ended up in a truck accident. Dos told me the person sent survived the accident, but Arnez died. I always disregard the stereotype that women gossip more than men because, within no time, Terrell found out. With people in Dos's circle and prisoners having such a fine line, it was inevitable that he would. But once again, Terrell proved why he was such a terrible cop. I pulled his letter out of my back pocket and reread it.

June 1, 2007

To: Cherese

I thought we had an agreement. I stayed at your place and you didn't tell anybody about the situation in Chicago and in turn, I didn't tell a certain someone about our relationship. Once again, you've tried my patience. Well, because you can't keep your word, I didn't keep mine. I wrote a letter to Memo and told him everything. Knowing my son, he's probably cursed you out by now. I got an empty envelope with two words on it and I bet you can guess what those two words were. The problem is while he's saying fuck me, I'm saying fuck you. I know what you did to Arnez. I don't know why he had to get involved when he hadn't done anything to you, but this is the only letter I'm writing to you. If you try that with me, remember I still have connections outside.

Kiss my ass,

Terrell

I rolled my eyes every time I read it. How many connections could he possibly have if he was rotting in prison once again? I cursed when I read the part about

Arnez. I'm sure Arnez and Terrell were introduced, with him being so close to Memo. I never told Terrell that Arnez was the person who gave the disease to me nor did I plan to. As long as the police couldn't make the connection between the two, I was cool. It wasn't my fault he died anyway. The truck accident wasn't supposed to happen and I wasn't the one who was responsible for him dying. The only person who knew about me and Arnez was Arnez and he wasn't talking.

Thinking this situation over and trying to figure out where I was going to get some money to move out of Golden's apartment, I picked up one of her cigarettes and, at the same time, the buzzer rang.

"Who is it?" I yelled into the intercom.

"¿Como estas, bonita?" Dos's familiar voice said.

I pressed the button to let him up and waited by the door. When I heard his footsteps, I looked out of the peephole to make sure he was alone.

"It's just me," he said.

I opened the door with the chain still on it. "How did you know where I was?"

He looked from right to left. "Can we have this conversation inside?"

"What conversation do we need to have?"

He looked shocked by my questions, as if it was normal to show up to someone's place who I didn't give a forwarding address. It was always hard to read Dos's facial expressions since he wore those damn contact lenses all the time. I always thought that was why he wore them. Today he was wearing bright yellow lenses with a black slit through them like a cat. "Ma, I just wanted to let you know that Memo is looking for you."

I closed the door and unlatched it. He slid in, and I immediately closed the door again. "What did he say?"

"Not much. You know Memo was always better about his game than Terrell. That's why I always wanted him to be my partner."

I nodded. "He still here?"

"Nah."

"You tell him where I was?"

He shook his head. "But if I figured it out, I'm sure he can."

"You could've called instead of visiting."

"I had some other business this way. Plus I wanted to make sure you were all right with the media hounding you and all."

I leaned against the wall. "That's the price I pay for hanging out with criminals."

"That's why you should hang out with me. I can show you the finer things in life."

I rolled my eyes. "I've bypassed the drug dealing men."

"I'm not a dealer. I'm a breaker."

"Who sells drugs and makes money the dirty way."

"You criticize the job, but you support the services."

The smirk on his face made me want to smack him. I looked around my mother's apartment and back to him. "And look where it got me. Staying with my mother, jobless, and with the cops down my throat."

He put his hand on the doorknob. "Well, that sounds like a personal problem. Just make sure they don't say my name."

"And if they do? What if the person who did this ends up telling? I don't want to get blamed for something I didn't ask for."

He turned the doorknob. "With the way Arnez drove, he was going to kill himself anyway." Women always thought Dos was cute, but to me, he just looked sneaky. "Anyway, let's keep this situation low-key, okay? I don't want to have to make another trip to Chicago and see our good friend, Memo." He opened the door, but before I closed it after him, I touched his arm.

"Dos, how did you know Arnez was a bad driver? You said you'd have to make another trip to Chicago."

He grinned again. "I've been there before. I didn't like Chicago though."

"Why not?"

His yellow eyes stared at me for a second before saying, "Got into a truck accident." He turned his back and walked down the hallway to the stairs. I closed the door and slid to the floor.

Chapter 21: Seleste

"Do you think he'll ever forgive me?" Cara asked me, sitting in the center of my bed with her arms wrapped around her knees.

"I don't think you're supposed to be sitting like that with chocolate in the box," I said, looking from her back to the television.

"Chocolate in the box?" She laughed.

"Which would you rather have? Chocolate in the box or bread in the oven. I'd rather have the chocolate."

"I'd rather have neither."

From the tone of her voice, I knew she meant that she'd rather not have been pregnant. I looked back at her as she stretched her legs and leaned her back against my wall. I didn't know what to say to her. I didn't know what to say to make anything better these days. When I heard the news about Arnez in the truck accident, I wasn't surprised. He always drove like he was a stunt double. But the news about him dying from AIDS caught me way offguard. Everybody hears news about things like that happening, but nobody expects it to be so close to home. When Cara called me after she came back from Atlanta, I was happy to hear that she and her baby didn't have it. Being a godmother had all the perks of watching a child grow up and avoiding the labor pains.

"You heard from Memo?" she asked me.

I shrugged. "You know, it's funny. He and I were together more when we weren't a couple than we are now. But, the situation with his father is crazy. Out of all of the people in the world, Terrell went right back to Cherese."

"I think it's odd that he keeps staying with his son's ex-girlfriend. Who does that kind of thing?"

"Well, Cherese was with him for over five years, so I can see the family getting pretty tight. It's not like he could stay with his cop friends after he was fresh out of jail."

"Did she ever say anything about Terrell while you were in New York?"

"She didn't say much of anything besides throwing out Memo's name from time to time. Me and that girl had no intentions of getting along, and that's how we left it."

"So now what is his mother doing?"

"Renee went back to her life. She had to. I mean, she can't sit around and be depressed forever, especially since now Terrell looks like he'll be in jail for a long time. He broke his probation, she's pressing charges against him, and then he got Cherese in trouble too for hiding him out."

"Yeah, I know. I saw it on the news. Did Memo?"

I nodded. "A couple of reporters called him asking stupid questions like how does it feel to find out there are police who are criminals." I rolled my eyes. "That's like asking how does it feel to see chocolate chips in cookies."

"Not all cops are like that."

I made a grunting noise at Cara. I'd had more than a few altercations in high school with cops stopping me for no reason to see my ID. I'd been in cars with both Jermaine and Memo, who were pulled over for no reason. I'd never wanted to meet Terrell for that reason alone. I was not a fan of police. When Memo told me he was working for a parole officer, I panicked, hoping he wasn't going to tell me he was going to the police force too. He was already graduating with a degree in Criminal Justice, and I assumed he'd go the lawyer route like me. But after the situation with his father, I was glad that Memo already had his graduation date set. The past few times I'd seen him, he looked so frazzled that there was no way he was going to class if it was still in session. Graduation day was the next week. He didn't even want to go. All he wanted to do lately was go to work. He was getting a little obsessed with his job, and I couldn't figure out why.

"Do you already have your outfit picked out for the big day?"

"Which day are you talking about?" I asked her.

She glared at me. "There's only one."

I gave her an apologetic expression. I kept trying to wrap my head around the wedding being canceled. When Jermaine told me he was going to propose to Cara, I wasn't even surprised. From the day those two met, I knew they were going to be together forever. I'd called Jermaine the day after the funeral to see if he was willing to give Cara another chance, but as hurt as he sounded, I knew it would be a long time. They'd both gotten their deposits back and returned everything with the wedding. Cecil picked up my maid of honor dress that I'd already paid for. It was the type of dress I could wear somewhere else anyway, so I had him ship it to me. I asked Cara if she would mind if I wore it to the graduation. She shrugged and said I might as well get some use out of it so I hung it on the back of my door.

With Memo dealing with his father, Jermaine keeping his distance from Cara, O not talking to anybody after Arnez's death, and Cara dealing with her pregnancy with only me, our crew was falling apart. I was hoping graduation would be one central location to get us back to the way we were, minus one.

*   *   *

I held the tip of my peach dress as I ran up the steps, looking around at all the white graduation gowns and caps. It didn't take me long to spot Jermaine and O leaning against a window. When they saw me, we hugged and I took a picture of the two. O wore a button-down gold and white shirt and khaki pants and Jermaine looked dapper in his black suit with a sky blue dress shirt and black tie.

"Looking good, fellas. Making a girl wish she was single again," I said, linking my arms through theirs with my back against the window.

"In six months, you'll be seeing me in my gown," O said to me. "You going to come to my graduation too?"

I traded glances with Jermaine. "Of course I'll come, O, just as soon as you realize college isn't home."

"Aw, that's cold," he said, pulling his arm away from me and laughing.

I leaned my head against O's shoulder. "I'm just playing. So how are you two doing?"

"I'm cool," Jermaine said. "Ready to get this thing going, you know. This suit is hot. I'm ready to put back on my jeans and a regular cap. I wish Arnez was here though." I felt O's shoulder stiffen from hearing Arnez's name. I linked my arm back into his, hoping our happy moment wouldn't disappear too fast.

"Hey, let's not think about that today. Think happy thoughts. Or, at least think nice thoughts about him. You know he'd be all frantic to graduate, hopping around and chanting. You know how much he liked to showboat."

Jermaine smiled. "Yeah, he did. Some of my ship is here already. They're talking about the party they're throwing in Calumet City."

"No problem. I'm there." I looked around for Memo. "Where's the third musketeer?"

O pointed to my right, and I saw Memo standing with his mother at a table. His graduation cap wasn't on, so I could see his freshly tapered cut with his shiny, short curls all over his head. He wore a diamond earring in his left ear and from under the unzipped gown, he rocked a pewter gray suit with a royal blue dress shirt. As I walked closer, I could see the blue and gray tie to match the blue tip in his alligator shoes. I grinned, thinking how absolutely fast he assimilated into Chicago fashion.

"Steve Harvey would give you a pat on the back right now," I said, reaching out to hug him. He turned to see me and beamed. I was shocked when he kissed me on the lips right in front of his mother and wrapped his arms around me tightly.

"I missed you," he whispered in my ear before turning around to look face-to-face at his mother. She looked pretty in her sleeveless blue ankle-length dress. There was a slight shimmer in it that complimented her clear sandals and silver make-up.

"You two would make a great prom date," I said laughing.

His mother looked at her son. "Yeah, he's cute enough to date me." She looked back at me and held out her hand. "It's so nice to see you again under better circumstances."

My eyes widened thinking about the last time we came in contact. "Yeah...I'm...."

"Uh uh, don't do that. That's in the past. That idiot is locked up now, and I'm getting a divorce for real this time. Starting my life fresh so I'm happy," she said to me. I looked from Renee to Memo and realized how much they looked alike, from the curly eyelashes to the wide nose. "Matter of fact, let's start over altogether. Hello, my name is Renee and you can call me Renee."

"I'd feel better calling you Mrs. Martin."

"And I'd wrestle you to the ground if you did," she said, winking at me. I had to laugh at that comment. She held her arms open. "I don't do handshakes, I do hugs." I unwrapped my arms from Memo and embraced her tiny frame. "It's good to meet the woman behind my son's smile."

I blushed and turned to see Memo grinning. "It's very nice to meet you too." Before our conversation could continue, we heard the director on the loudspeaker telling the graduates to line up. I turned to walk away and Memo pulled the back of my dress.

"No kiss for good luck?" he whispered to me.

I squinted my eyes at him. "You're graduating regardless. Why are you in such a good mood?"

"Can't I be in a good mood just from seeing you?"

"Something else is up," I said.

"Kiss me."

"Your mom is right there."

"I don't give a damn. I'm grown. She probably thinks we're going to do what we do right after graduation."

I laughed loudly. He cut me off by kissing me. I peeked out of one eye to see Renee grinning her butt off at us. Public displays of affection, one of my favorite things in the world. People started bumping into us trying to get by.

"Get a room," somebody yelled jokingly in the crowd. I recognized the voice and saw that it was O saying it. Memo pushed him playfully and followed him.

"Let's go, before they kick us out of here," Renee said, touching my arm. "Did you come with anybody?"

"Yeah, I came with my friend Cara. Have you met her yet? She's sitting in the front row. You want to sit with us?"

"We might be close to you. My son, Jeremiah, is already saving me a seat with a couple of our relatives. You want to meet them?"

"I know Jeremiah already. I actually met him before I met Memo." I explained how I met Jeremiah on a train one day and didn't realize he was Memo's younger brother until I saw his photo at Memo's place. Memo and I joked later about how Jeremiah was annoyed when I started talking to Memo on the phone while I was away. It turned out Jeremiah had a slight crush on me, never mind him being almost a decade younger than me. I found Cara sitting by the front of the rows of graduation seats near the spot where the Criminal Justice majors would be. She looked up to see who the woman was next to me, and I introduced them. Renee wasn't lying because she leaned down to hug Cara.

"I'm going to have a bunch of people by my house after this. You two are invited," Renee said. "I'll look for you all after the ceremony to take pictures. You're coming, right?" Cara and I agreed to attend, and Renee waved and walked away.

I sat down next to Cara. "You all right?"

"Yeah, I'll be okay. It just feels weird not to be walking up to Jermaine to congratulate him and not being engaged anymore. I feel like we're back to where we were when he went to California."

"You can still congratulate him. Hell, I couldn't stand Arnez and I went to their frat party when he crossed."

"Seleste, you shouldn't speak badly about the dead."

I shrugged. "The truth is the truth. I think it's messed up that he did that to Anita. I don't blame her for acting up at the funeral. The rest of his groupies at the funeral needed to know what was going on."

"The rest of his groupies?"

"I wasn't talking about you. Calm down. I was talking about Anita and everybody else. He should've taken responsibility and not done that to Anita. Regardless of how much I don't like Lisa, I feel sorry for her. I would never want to get news like that about you or Jermaine. It's hard enough on Anita, but then her friends have to deal with that kind of news too. If you'd have told me that you came back from the doctor's office and your baby had..." I looked around to make sure no one was paying attention to our conversation. The bleachers were so packed with people snapping photos and talking amongst themselves so I figured they weren't listening to what I had to say, but I still spoke a little lower. "If you'd have told me Arnez gave you that, then I'd have killed him myself."

156

"Seleste, let's just talk about something else. I know you didn't like Arnez, but now my child doesn't have a father."

"Arnez wasn't going to be a father to that kid regardless."

"That time I wasn't even talking about Arnez. If Jermaine hadn't've found out about Arnez, he'd still be around."

"Arnez or Jermaine?"

"I can't help what happened to Arnez. That was his fault. But I wish I'd have not gotten pregnant. That's for sure."

I shrugged. "Shit happens."

She opened her mouth to respond but changed her mind and turned around. "Seleste, there are some things you'll just never understand."

I looked at her. "Are we talking about Arnez or Jermaine?"

She crossed her legs and laid her arms on top of them. "Both."

"Cara, nobody can bring Arnez back. That car accident was unexpected, but that man was going to die regardless. That's just the truth of the matter. I have no sympathy for him. It was no reason that he had to take other people down with him because he didn't want to take personal responsibility for his actions. A billion commercials about condoms, a trillion commercials about black people getting this disease the most, and motherfuckers still think they're invincible. It doesn't make any sense to me, and to top it all off, they're too immature to take the time to take care of themselves before others have to deal with the same thing. If people would just put on condoms…"

Cara pinched me. "Shut up. You're getting loud."

I opened my mouth to speak again, but the music started and I saw a group of graduates come out. I leaned over to her and said, "Okay, I've said my peace about Arnez, but if you want Jermaine back, he's still alive and breathing. You're going to have to work hard to get him back because he's hurt, but he still loves you. So, I'd suggest you take Renee up on her offer to go to that dinner because Jermaine will probably be there."

She didn't answer me. Instead, she pulled her camera out of its bag and aimed it. I turned to see Memo coming down the aisle. I yelled out his name, he turned to me, struck a b-boy pose, and Cara snapped the photo.

"He's so silly," Cara remarked.

"That's what I love about him," I said. Cara's head whipped around at the same time I covered my mouth. I didn't know where that came from, but now that it was out of my mouth, I didn't want to take it back. "Don't tell him I said that."

"Now who really needs to talk to somebody and let them know how they feel?" she asked me.

I stared ahead and didn't make eye contact. One of the professors started a speech and in the middle of her talking, I felt someone scooting me over. I looked over to see Jeremiah trying to squeeze between me and a lady I sat next to.

"What's up?" I whispered to him, putting my arm around his shoulder.

"You look cute," he said.

I smiled at him and checked out his maroon, white, and gray button-down shirt and khakis. It was still taking me time to get use to him without the dreadlocks, but he looked handsome either way. I knew Renee's phone would be blowing up soon since Jeremiah would be starting high school in the fall, unless it already was. "Thank you. You do too."

"Did you hear the news?" he asked me.

"What news?" I asked.

He got ready to answer me but then looked up and pointed. I turned to see the professor announce that the valedictorian, Travis Martin, would be the next speaker. I was surprised to see Memo was standing onstage. I'd taken classes with Memo, but we'd never really discussed grades. I grinned from ear-to-ear like a proud parent and for the first time noticed the cloth around his neck that distinguished him from the rest of the graduates. He didn't have that on when I went to see him upstairs. Jeremiah and I stood up to cheer for him onstage and were joined by Renee, Jermaine, Cara, and O yelling his name out and clapping over the other polite clappers.

"Thank you everybody, especially the loud ones to my right," Memo said, looking our way. A few people laughed in the audience. "Well, first I'd like to say to the graduates that I'm so glad this is over. We worked long and hard to get to this point and it feels good to be able to graduate from college." A couple of people whistled and shouted "yeah." "Historically black colleges and universities are fighting to stay around and gain support so I hope that when we all graduate and are alumni members, we continue to support the school to make sure it's still as successful and enjoyable for other students as it was for us. Not only am I going to remember the classes I took, the grades I busted my butt for, and the professors who helped me in my path, I'm going to miss my friends, this campus, and obviously the parties. But more importantly, I'm going to miss the innocence we'll lose entering the real world. It's a big transition to leave college where you're basically concentrating on grades and trying to deal with being in a twelve by twelve to supporting yourself, moving out of Mom's house for good, children, marriage, careers, and all of the rest of that stuff. Some of us are already there. Some of us are in for a big awakening. But whatever you do, appreciate life because some of us didn't get that opportunity." Memo cleared his throat. "When you leave school, remember those who helped you succeed and don't take anyone for granted. And make sure that you are there for your friends and family who will need you as they grow too. Congratulations, Class of 2007."

A bunch of people in the Criminal Justice department stood up and cheered. I stood up with Cara and Jeremiah to cheer just as loudly as when he was introduced and looked over to see tears coming from Renee's eyes. She saw me looking at her, touched her heart, and smiled. I made a mental note to call my parents when I got home. I hadn't talked to them in awhile with all the craziness going on. I looked over at Cara, who had tears coming out of her eyes too.

"Graduations make everybody cry, huh?" I asked her.

She sniffed and looked at me. "Memo is so lucky. His mother is here on his special day. You know my mother didn't even call me to ask why my wedding was canceled. My grandfather left her a voicemail message, and I haven't heard from her yet."

"Her loss," I said, putting my arm around her. "I know I'll be at your graduation, whenever you decide to pick a major."

She laughed. "Hey, I've stuck to my art major."

I rolled my eyes. "Yeah, for now. A whole year. You'll graduate when O does."

She muffed my head, and I laughed. Looking down at Jeremiah, he was still grinning as Memo walked back to his seat. After a speech from a Magna Cum Laude student and a couple more professors, names were called and we all cheered when we saw people we knew. People yelled out Jermaine's name when he was called. His radio show had really taken off. I knew he was going to be big one day, if not from deejaying, he'd definitely go into music production. When the ceremony was over, Jeremiah walked out with the two of us, and we met Renee and the group she was with outside on the grass. Jermaine came out with his gown wrapped over his arm, his graduation cap in hand, and a basketball cap on his head. Memo walked with him with his gown hanging over his shoulder. I looked around for O but he was nowhere in sight. I turned to ask Renee if she'd seen him at all during the graduation, but she immediately pushed Memo and I together to take pictures. Our crew teased the two of us when he kissed me on the cheek in one photo. Renee introduced the group she was with as Memo's family from Brooklyn and Long Island. Some of Jermaine's family members walked over to say hello to me. I noticed they avoided Cara and she noticed too because she moved away from Jermaine's family to stand next to Arnez's younger sister, Corleen. My eyes widened to see her here. I didn't think she'd come now that her brother wasn't in the graduation. She walked over to Memo and Jermaine to congratulate them with balloons and a flower. I'd never met her, but from the way they greeted her, I'm sure they had. Memo introduced Corleen to his crew and asked her what she was doing later on.

"O and I are going to the cemetery for a little while," she explained. "He's in the car now. He said to tell you all that he'd meet up with you later, but we just wanted to...you know, put flowers on Arnez's grave." Jermaine and Memo exchanged a few words with her and Memo turned to Renee and me to tell us he was going to ride with Corleen. Jermaine declined on going and headed over to his family. I looked over to see what Cara wanted to do.

"I'm going to go with Memo and Corleen too," she said to me. I nodded at her. "This will be my last time going there. I hate cemeteries, but I just feel like he deserves for people to come today. This was supposed to be his special day too, you know," she said to me. I felt my stomach flop a little. I had been too busy placing blame on him for what he did to Anita to acknowledge that other

161

people were hurting as well. Regardless of what Arnez did or how mean he could be sometimes, it was obvious that Cara still cared about him a great deal. She always had. Not as much as she did Jermaine, but enough. I wanted O to come over and take photos with us, but I hesitated to follow them to the parking lot. O was definitely taking his friend's death the hardest of all of us. My eyes watered a little thinking about how I'd react if I were in O's position and it had been my best friends who died. I wouldn't care no matter how wrong they were living. What would stand out to me was the good memories I had with them while they were alive.

"Baby, are you okay?" Renee asked me, rubbing my arm. I sniffed and realized that I was crying. She smiled at me. "I cried all through the ceremony, especially when Memo got onstage to do his speech. I'm proud of him too. He's a great man, isn't he?" I nodded my head, not wanting to tell her the real reason I was crying. "Come on, let's go. Did you drive?" I nodded to her and pointed in the direction of the parking lot where my car was. I didn't really want to ride alone so I was relieved when Renee asked if a couple of Memo's relatives could ride with me.

The three of us made small talk in the car and took the scenic route there so they could see some of the city. I drove downtown to let them see the Magnificent Mile, the Buckingham Fountain, the Sears Tower, and the John Hancock building. They nodded their heads with approval as I drove past Navy Pier so they could see the ferris wheel and commented that the city looked just like the postcards. I smiled and nodded. I couldn't see myself living anywhere but here. I turned around to get back onto Lake Shore Drive headed to I-94.

One of his cousins, Tweet, looked in the backseat at Memo's godbrother, Red, and said, "Aren't you glad Cherese's crazy ass couldn't come to his graduation?"

162

Red groaned. "Man, I'm so glad Memo stopped going out with that girl. I couldn't stand her."

Tweet turned to me. "You're cool though. We like you."

I smiled at her. "I'm glad you like me. Hopefully I don't do anything wrong and end up the topic of conversation with the next chick."

Tweet patted my leg. "Nah, you're good. Auntie Renee doesn't like everybody, and she'll tell you if she doesn't like you too, but she likes you though." Tweet turned to talk to Red. "She's handling Terrell's arrest real good too. She claims she's going to divorce him this time. I know she won't. Even when she cheated on him back in the day and got pregnant with Jeremiah, they still got back together. Him not following parole ain't good enough to divorce him. She'll be back."

I raised an eyebrow, first because I had no idea that Jeremiah wasn't Memo's biological brother, and second because I wondered if they knew the real reason Terrell fled Chicago. There had only been a couple of news reports about Terrell before the media moved on to something else, but from what I'd read and seen on the news, no one had mentioned Terrell trying to rape Renee. From the way Tweet was talking, Renee must've not shared this information with her family either. I was going to have to ask Memo later how they managed to keep that out of the limelight, especially since Terrell already had a history.

"You know Cherese wasn't leaving the Bronx anyway, not with Terrell in jail. She's going to follow that man around like she did Memo," Red said.

My mouth dropped. "What are you talking about?" I felt a sudden chill in the car.

"You didn't know?" Red asked me.

"Know what?" I asked.

"I'm sorry. I thought Memo would've told you by now," Red said.

"Told me what?" I said.

"Aw man, my fault. Well, it's too late now so I might as well tell you. Cherese and Terrell use to mess around."

I held the steering wheel with both hands and tried not to crash. "Terrell is Memo's father."

"No shit, Sherlock," Tweet said, laughing.

"Does Memo know this?" I asked.

"Yeah, we were trying to tell him that way back when Terrell moved in with her. He wasn't trying to hear us. I don't know if he believes it now though, but Renee does. She was talking about it when we were at the graduation, calling him a cradle robber. He's a loser anyway. Auntie can do better for herself. He was a pig. What'd she expect?" Tweet explained.

"Wow," was all I could say. Red and Tweet informed me that Cherese moved out of her apartment to let Terrell stay there, but Cherese's mother called the cops on him. I knew Terrell was in jail from the news, but I wondered where Cherese was and why Memo hadn't told me any of this. I felt stupid for telling Cara I loved him. Obviously if he loved me, he wouldn't have kept something like this from me so I definitely wasn't going to tell him anything like that. I parked in front of the house, and the three of us got out and went in to see balloons all over the living room and a cake on the dining room table with dishes of baked chicken, butter noodles with pepper, collard greens, hot water cornbread, fresh rolls, and macaroni and cheese. The smell of chicken was making me nauseous, but everything else smelled great. My stomach started to grumble. Tweet and Red joined Renee in the kitchen while I sat down with the rest of his relatives at the graduation and eyed the photos on the walls. This was my second time being at his mother's house and I hadn't taken the time to look at the place the first time I was there considering the circumstances. I saw photos of Memo and Jeremiah in elementary and high school, but the two photos that caught my attention the most was a shot of Memo at senior prom. I'd know those dreads anywhere. Cherese was his date, and I couldn't deny how beautiful a couple they were. She wore a sleeveless beige dress with jewels along the v-neck line. Her arms were just as muscular then as they were during our internship. I looked down at my own thicker arms and wondered if I could've taken her. I shook that thought away. How childish of me to think that, but I'd never been so protective of a man in my life.

The second photo was a picture of the four of them: Jeremiah, Memo, Renee, and Terrell. The mug shot of Terrell I'd seen on television wasn't flattering of course, but this photo of him was a dead ringer for what Memo would look like as he got older. I looked at the goatee, low cut, and confident smile on his face. Minus the chipped tooth, this was Memo from head to toe in a slightly taller man's body. No matter how much of a pretty boy Memo looked like, that tooth gave him a little edge. I remembered what Tweet said in the car about Jeremiah, and from the looks of it, Jeremiah looked nothing like Terrell. It made sense that that wasn't his biological son, but I still wondered why Memo never mentioned that.

"I like that photo too much to take it down. Been meaning to though," Renee said to me. I looked over to see her sitting next to me. I hadn't noticed that the other people in the room had moved to the dining room. From the clicking of silverware and conversation, it sounded like they were getting ready to eat. "Hungry?"

I shook my head no.

"Girl, I cooked all that food. You better eat my food. What's wrong with it? You a vegetarian or something?"

I smiled. "I am, but that's not why I'm not hungry."

"Hey, the macaroni doesn't have meat in it and neither does the bread or noodles. You got baby-making hips, honey. Had to get them somewhere."

"You are too much."

"I know it," she said, slapping my leg. "Let's go get you something nonmeat to eat, okay?"

I stood up and she got ready to lead me to the dining room. "Renee, can I ask you a question?"

She turned to look at me. "Sure."

"I know you may not want to talk about Mr. Martin, but I just have a question. How do you think Memo is taking this all in? When I see him, he's usually grinning or changing the subject. He doesn't really talk about it with me. I heard about Cherese from Red and Tweet though. I'm sorry that happened."

Renee rolled her eyes. "Bunch of big mouths. Don't you believe that New York is too big for folks to be in each other's lives. All those people there and some of them act like they live in some small town all up in each other's business." She shook her head. "But to answer your question, I think Memo will be all right. Memo is a hothead, but he's not that way all the time. Mad one minute and not mad the next. He's like me. I could be furious about something for two seconds and by the third, I've let it go."

"But what happened to you was huge."

"No doubt about it, but I can't carry that in my heart forever. I moped around for a couple months, but one day I prayed and realized one very important thing. I lived through it. So I have to keep living, you know? Life is strange that way. If it happened, it had to be a reason for it. All Terrell did was remind me why I needed to divorce him the first time and why I won't give in again. He's in prison now anyway, so I'm not worried about it. If he or Cherese ever step foot in Chicago again, I'll shoot them both where they stand. So, ready to get that food?"

I blinked a couple of times and wondered whether I should laugh or run at how matter-of-fact Renee said her remark about shooting Terrell. "Yes, I'm hungry now that I'm scared to say no to you again."

She threw her head back and howled with laughter. "You should be. Now make sure you treat my son right and you and I will be okay." She patted my back and I followed her, looking back at the photo of Terrell again. I was wrong the first time when I thought he and Memo looked alike. There was one major difference. Terrell's eyes looked tired and angry in contrast to the smile on his face. Memo's eyes on the photo and in person always looked sexy. No matter how mad he was, his face was charming, like he could talk a turtle into walking out of its shell just by winking at it. I hoped Memo would never become a cop and end up with the same stressed out look in his eyes. Terrell looked like he'd seen too much and given up completely on helping out. I wondered if all cops felt that way at one point and time, or were there still good ones out there.

About ten minutes later, I heard Memo yelling, "Where's the food?" I turned to see him walking in with Cara and O. Corleen didn't come, and for the first time, I remembered that Jermaine wasn't there. I dialed my phone to call him and see if he was planning to come over, but stopped when I saw him come through the opposite entrance of the dining room. Memo's eyes were on the chicken, but he looked up to see me sitting at the other end of the table and climbed over Tweet and Red to get to me. He leaned down and kissed my lips. "Sorry I had to leave you with my family. I hope you still want to be with me after meeting these psychos."

"Uh uh, how are you going to call us psychos like that?" Tweet interjected.

"And nosey as hell too," Memo added.

"Memo, Seleste is cool. You should marry that one before she gets away," Red said.

"Took the words right out of my mouth," Renee said.

Memo looked from his cousin to his mother and back to me. "Damn, what'd you do to these people? Pay one of their bills?" I looked up at him and burst out laughing. Typical Memo. Always with a comeback.

Chapter 22: Memo

The perk of doing clerical work for a parole officer is they hate paperwork with a passion. The problem with it is that they're are also very protective of anything they find on a case, and are disgruntled about having to constantly watch out for the same activity. Looking up information on Cherese proved pointless. I'd watched the news and read the paper detailing Terrell's probation issues. My mother and I had spoken with a couple of his old friends to make sure that journalists knew nothing about the restraining order she placed against him. He warned us that if she filed a case against him for trying to rape her, the media would snag that up immediately, especially since he was an officer. Not only mainstream news, but minority-owned newspapers would eat that up to detail that not only were cops in New York catching heat for racial profiling but were breaking other laws as well, not like no one knew it, but Terrell would've been proof. I couldn't blame them for doing so, but I didn't want my family to be the example. My father's friend explained that if she settled that case out of court, Terrell's rap sheet wouldn't have that on it, but because he didn't follow probation, he'd still be incarcerated. As soon as Renee found out that he'd have to stay in jail and in New York if he was released, she agreed to settle. She also took the sweater off and slowly started to relax. Cases like these usually took at least a year to be handled but the intensity of it and by Terrell being who he was, the police wanted this over as quickly as possible to take the limelight off of them.

I'd read and reread Terrell's letter so many times I knew it by heart, but at the end of the day, what was done was done. If I went to the Bronx and set foot on her mother's door, that wouldn't change what she did with my father. I'd finally gotten her to stop bugging me about getting back together. My mother was now safe in her own home, and I didn't have to worry about Terrell screwing anything up in Chicago. I thought she was going to turn into a hermit for the rest of her life, but she was going back to her usual self. Jeremiah was doing all right in school regardless of the circumstances. Seleste and I were happy, and I'd just graduated. It was time to get my grown man on.

"How you doing, Memo? Good seeing you." I turned around to see Red opening the screen door and sitting on the porch.

I grinned. I'd taken the suit jacket off and hung it up in Jeremiah's coat closet. I unbuttoned the wrists of my dress shirt and rolled the sleeves up. The sun was out, and I could hear some little girls jumping rope down the street. "I'm doing good. Just enjoying today, you know."

"That's cool. You know some people on the block got things to say about you though."

"Haters come around like weeds. No matter how much you try to dig them out, they always grow back."

"Yeah, that's true. But there's something I thought you needed to know."

"I already know Cherese is hiding out at her mother's house."

"You know she got arrested, right?"

I frowned at my godbrother. "What'd she do to get arrested?"

"She got arrested for letting Terrell stay at her house. Guilty by association."

I raised an eyebrow. "That's what she gets. I don't care. I got Seleste, and I'm not concerned about what that girl does. Let her do her. If she wants to be with my father no matter how screwed up that is, nothing surprises me about her. After you've been around somebody for that long and they do something like that to you, you don't really need them in your life so why bother trying to rationalize

170

what they do." I stood up, ready to go back inside and find Seleste. This conversation was getting to be too much like gossip, and I was not feeling that. I touched the handle of the screen door.

"So it's okay what she did to Arnez?"

I let the door handle go and turned around. "Excuse me?"

"You know, your friend in the car accident."

"What does Arnez have to do with Cherese?"

"She was responsible for that."

"What are you talking about?" I asked, sitting back down on the stoop.

"Word on the street is Cherese sent one of Dos's people up here to handle Arnez."

"Why would Cherese do that?"

Red shrugged. "See, that's what I can't figure out. Cherese never came to Chicago so she can't have any beef with anybody up here."

"She came here once."

"When?"

"Last winter."

"Oh," he said. He leaned forward. "Did she get into it with anybody here?"

"Not Arnez."

He smirked at me. "You sure about that?"

"Positive."

He held up his hands like he was surrendering. "Okay, maybe I got my story wrong. Just telling you what I heard."

"The next time you hear something, do me a favor."

"What's that?"

"Keep that shit to yourself." I stormed up the steps and yanked the screen door open. I saw Seleste talking in the corner with Cara, and Jermaine was across the room conversing with Jeremiah. My mother walked my way, and I stormed past her and upstairs to Jeremiah's room to grab

171

my car keys. I'd left my car here and rode with my mother to the graduation ceremony. I hopped back down the stairs and headed out of the door to my car and saw someone come running up behind me.

"Memo, where are you going?" I heard Jermaine yell. I waved for him to head in the direction of my car. "Give me two seconds." He came back out, holding his frat jacket in his hand and closed the door. Jogging to the passenger side, as soon as his feet hit the car floor, I sped off almost swiping the side mirror of the car in front of mine.

Chapter 23: Cara

I looked from the slammed door to Seleste and our eyes trailed over to a young guy who'd come from the porch with Memo. He walked over to whisper to a light-skinned girl with blonde and sandy brown microbraids, and she stood up to run to the window. We heard tires burn down the street, and I walked to the window. Memo's car was gone. From the way Jermaine ran out the door, I knew he was with him.

Renee stormed over to the guy and yanked him up by the back of his neck. If the situation wasn't so intense, I'd have probably laughed. Renee was one tough woman. From the way she moved, it looked like she should've been the cop, not her husband. The two of them went into the kitchen. I watched as other people slowly trickled past us and tried to listen to the conversation. I copied and leaned against the kitchen door.

"How do you know that?" Renee hissed.

"You know how people talk. You know you can't keep secrets over there. Dos likes to talk too much. He's too much of a show-off. His car is flashy. The contacts. He claims he's big time on the streets, but he's selling like a petty dealer. I knew it wouldn't take long for word to spread about this one though. He came back with his brand new car all banged up, lying about it being a car accident in Jersey. One person started talking and the word spread."

"But that doesn't make any sense. Cherese doesn't even know Arnez."

My eyes bugged out at the mention of Arnez.

"Well, she had to know him. There had to be a reason why she got Dos to come here to fight him."

"So how did the car accident happen?"

173

"I think that was an accident. It was never supposed to reach that point. But, you know, I hear Arnez isn't so great of a driver."

I nodded my head remembering countless times that Arnez had gotten speeding tickets. At one point, he had a ticket collection to match his bra collection. Seleste complained once about how she got a speeding ticket and freaked out enough to stop driving her car until it was paid for, but Arnez laughed off his tickets like they were nothing.

"So what is that girl doing now?" Renee asked.

"She's still hiding at her mother's house," Red replied.

"Where is Memo going?"

"I have no idea."

"Look, Red, I don't appreciate you coming in my house and starting this shit. Today was supposed to be my son's day to relax. He was finally letting that whole situation go and now here you go starting stuff. Why do you think I made him come with me to Chicago? I wanted him to get away from all of that drama."

"Are you kidding me? Chicago doesn't have a halo over it. Stuff happens here too. You'll never see a blank newspaper here."

"But one thing Chicago does not have is you. Or Tweet. Or Dos. Grow up, boy. You're almost eighteen years old and still gossiping like a school girl. If you paid more attention to your grades and less time worried about the streets, you'd be graduating this year like your godbrother. Get out of my house right now, and do not call Memo to see where he went. Just leave. Go back to New York and keep shit up there, but you have got to get out of my house."

A group of people scrambled away from the door, and I headed out the front door. Not even two minutes later, Red slumped outside too.

"She's making me wait out here for the cab to come," he said to me. I guess he realized we were all listening. Twenty or so pair of footsteps running from a door isn't exactly a great way to sneak away.

"Red, I need to ask you a question about what you said about Cherese."

"Renee told me not to say anything else."

I leaned back against the stoop. "Well, Renee ain't out here and I am. So tell me, what really happened with Arnez? Better yet, what are people where you're at saying happened to Arnez?"

He squinted his eyes at me. "Why are you so concerned?"

"I just want to know."

"Why do you want to know?"

"If I don't find out from you, I will find out from Memo, so the choice is yours."

Red looked me up and down. "What do I get for telling you?"

I opened my mouth to answer him and saw a checkerboard out of the corner of my eye. I turned to see a cab with that design. "No information is worth all that. Enjoy your ride to the airport." He turned to see the car and descended down the stairs.

At the bottom of the steps, he turned to me and said, "I'll be seeing you soon."

"Why is that?"

"If Memo comes back to New York, the next funeral will probably be his."

I stared down at Red, wondering what would make him give Memo information that could possibly endanger him. Who needs enemies when he has family like that? He looked out the window at me as the driver drove off and the front door opened.

"Cara, I'm getting ready to leave. Are you riding with me?"

I turned around to see Seleste standing in the doorway with her keys in her hand. "Yeah. You headed home?"

"Nope, I'm headed to Memo's place and hope he's not about to make a stupid mistake." I stood up and winced when I felt pain in my stomach. Slowly, I sat back down.

She jogged down the stairs towards me. "Are you all right?"

I shook my head and reached up for her arm. "I'm good. Just a little dizzy. I think I'm just light-headed from not eating all day. Nervous about Jermaine and then upset after going to see Arnez at the cemetery. Just some stress."

"Well, I'll take you home then and keep going." She pulled me up from the steps slowly, and I started walking to her car.

"Nah, I want to go. I have to know the full story."

Seleste tried not to drive in her usual maniacal way, but it didn't work. She lasted four blocks before she started cutting people off, running stop signs, and cursing up a storm. She may not have liked Arnez all that much, but both of them had to have learned to drive at the same stunt double school. When we pulled up in front of Memo's apartment, she jumped out first and ran around to the side parking lot to see if his car was there. It still was. We followed a tenant through the security door. Hopping up two steps at a time, Seleste got to his door long before I did on the elevator. By the time I got to the top, the door was already open and Jermaine was talking frantically.

"Memo, think clearly, dawg. Why would your godbrother tell you something like that unless he was trying to set you up? If he was really in your corner, he would've handled that situation regardless of you being there. Instead, he came all the way here to tell you about it," Jermaine said.

Memo walked back and forth putting jeans in a suitcase. "Why would he handle something that didn't have anything to do with him? Red was looking out for me by telling me. You mean to tell me you don't want to go too? That's your friend. Matter of fact, Arnez is supposed to be your brother. I bet if I told anybody else in your frat about this, they'd be on the plane with me."

"Don't play yourself. You're not going there to defend Arnez's honor. You're going to attack Cherese. All you're going to do is keep the circle going. You mess her up and then the cops come for you. Then both you and your father are in the system. You already lucked out once. Do you really want to do this again? Think about that. Do you really feel like dealing with that? Better yet, imagine what they'll do to you if you go in there wilding out. You can't be a superhero all the time." He turned to look at Seleste. "Will you talk some sense into this fool?"

She looked from Memo throwing in shoes and shirts and back to Jermaine. "I need somebody to tell me what's going on. I only heard a piece of the story after you two stormed out." Memo continued to pack while Jermaine filled us in. Memo's plan was to go to the Bronx, confront Cherese, and make her admit that she was responsible for Arnez's death. I sat down in his desk chair and held my head. I watched them argue and scream, and the more Memo walked back and forth, the more I started seeing two of him. I leaned my elbow against his laptop, accidentally pressing some keys. At the sound of the beeping, the yelling stopped.

"Cara, babe, what's wrong?" Memo asked me.

I winced. "Will somebody please...?" I opened my mouth to speak again and blacked out.

Chapter 24: Cherese

"I can't do it anymore. I can't deal with all this drama you and Memo have," Golden said to me.

I sat up on her futon and wiped the sleep out of my eyes. "What are you talking about?"

"You have to get out of my house. I can't even go to work without people asking me 50,000 questions about that boy's father. You have until I come home from work to get out of here. I don't care where you go, but you have to get out of here. Just let the police know where you go, and if you don't, I will. And that man better not be sending letters to my house like he did the last time. I let him stay with us before until you moved out, and I'm not going through that again. He will not set foot in my house again. Me and Rod need privacy."

I didn't respond. Instead I laid back down on the bed with my eyes closed. A few minutes later, I smelled her cooking breakfast but knew she wouldn't ask me if I wanted any. I heard her taking a shower but knew she'd use up all the hot water. I heard her walk out of the door, and I knew she wouldn't say goodbye. That was a typical response from Golden. She was the reason why I clung so hard to Memo. He was the only one who seemed to care about me, and the reason I even attempted to try to get a law degree. While I did the internship with Seleste, I realized I was bored with the idea of it and only following along because I knew Memo would be proud that I did. I hadn't been in school since, and the money from that internship was running out quickly.

I got up and got dressed, packing my few things into a bag. I went into the kitchen to cook something for breakfast but everything in there had Golden's name written on a label. I shrugged and pulled a bagel from her package. I saw the piece of thread fall to the floor and

rolled my eyes at her trying to catch me in the act of eating
her food. Squatting down to pick up the thread, I looked up
at the calendar on my mother's kitchen wall, concentrating
on the date that I'd written Memo's graduation time. I really
wanted to see him graduate. I was proud of him for getting
out of the neighborhood to better himself. I knew if he
stayed in New York, he'd end up following in either his
friends' footsteps or his father's. I wondered what he
looked like on graduation and if he still wore the same
cologne as the last time I'd seen him at that Chicago hotel.
I wondered how he would react most to the letter I wrote
him though. I tapped the bottom of the envelope on the
counter and pondered on whether I should mail it. If he
knew what happened, maybe he'd understand my side of
the story. But if his attitude was the same, I knew he'd be
back. The problem with Memo was that he was convinced
that he was invincible. If he set foot in front of my door, I'd
try to talk him out of his anger. But if he set foot on Dos's
door, I knew Dos would kill him, and Memo knew it too.
Memo's father being a cop was a gift and a curse for him.
By Terrell being a police officer, Memo was always being
provoked and people were constantly wondering whether
he'd tell on his friends' actions. Memo never did though.
He lived by the street code of no snitching. When I found
out Terrell was just as bad as the criminals Memo and I
hung out with, I wondered if Memo really did live by that
rule out of principle or because he simply didn't have to.
His father was the person to snitch to but seemed to be
content not knowing a damn thing about solving crime.

On the other hand, Terrell was no fool. He knew that
Memo and Jeremiah both would have to deal with
unnecessary drama because even after moving to Long
Island, those two always came back to their old stomping
grounds in Brooklyn. When Terrell tried to talk them out of
visiting, to no avail, he decided to go another route. He
taught them how to shoot. Memo use to have a body

target on his wall. By about the fourth week of shooting, Memo had improved his range. I'd visit his home on the weekends when I had time to travel without it being late at night, and I'd joke about never making him mad. The target on his wall had eight shots by the x mark. So if Memo came looking for Dos, I knew he wasn't coming empty handed.

I didn't really understand Dos. He'd come to my apartment that one time to tell me not to say a word, but gotten too caught up in his own accidental victory of getting rid of Arnez. Now he thought he was some big hitman. Although I was supposed to stay close to home, I wasn't necessarily on house arrest. The cops could not pin anything on me besides being sympathetic enough to let my ex-boyfriend's father live with me and get his life together. So, I'd talk to people around my mom's house and see what the news was. Even though Brooklyn and the Bronx were two different boroughs, communication didn't die from distance. If you really wanted to know something, it was nothing to find out, especially if too many people knew it. The saying about the only way to keep a secret is to tell no one is so underrated.

Memo hadn't called me in over two weeks. I was hoping that meant that he didn't know what had happened and gave up. But when graduation rolled around and I bumped into Red, Memo's godbrother, on the train, I got a little worried. Red, being young, dumb, and trying to be cool, had started rolling with Dos. Sidekicks always wanted to be cooler than they really were, and I knew Red had a big mouth because he was the one to tell Memo's mother what happened to get Memo locked up. He was the one who ran around the neighborhood talking about how Memo got his tooth chipped. He was also the one who made a point of telling people that Memo was running away to Chicago, disregarding the drama going around with his father. When he told me he was invited to the graduation, I was dumbstruck. How could an instigator like him be invited and not me? I'd put up with Memo for well over five years and tried to rekindle our relationship through college too. Hell, I kept my hands off of Seleste just so Memo wouldn't think I was some crazy ex-girlfriend. And this was the thanks I got. No invitation. I'd called the station repeatedly to see if the invitation came to my apartment, which I still wasn't allowed to go into until this case blew over.

I picked up the phone and dialed nine digits of Memo's number, but hesitated on the very last one. I hung the phone up and leaned against my suitcase sitting between my legs. I couldn't stay here. I closed my eyes and hung up the phone again. Tapping the letter in my hand, I headed to the bathroom to get my toothbrush. Opening the medicine cabinet, I saw the pills I was told to take by the doctor who confirmed that I had AIDS. My mother never even asked me about them. She made sure I didn't touch her bacon, but somehow newfound pill containers weren't of interest to her.

I stared at the medicine for a few seconds, pondering on swallowing them all. Too typical. I wasn't willing to cheat myself anymore out of life than I already had. I closed the cabinet, walked back into the kitchen, and pulled out a pen and a piece of paper.

Life
Is Short
Time Is Necessary

Dear Memo,

I know you've seen the stories about your father and him staying with me. I want to apologize for doing what I did with him. He wrote me a letter and told me he'd already told you about us. I would've liked to tell you

first, but this shouldn't have been something I did at all.
At the time, I felt that Terrell was the only thing I had
left so I held tight. I now know that wasn't the best
decision. Neither was having sex with your friend,
Arnez. I was just trying to reach out to you, but I
chose the worst way possible to do it by trying to touch
all of those around you. Please let Seleste know that
I'm sorry for any trouble I may have caused. Please
send my apologies to Renee for helping to tear up her
relationship with her husband. I didn't appreciate it
when Seleste was in my way, so I know Renee hates that
I had a relationship with her husband.
Although Dos does not see the wrongs in what he's done,
it is my responsibility to apologize for what happened to
Arnez. Regardless of what Arnez did to me, it was not
my place to have someone come to Chicago to fight him.
I should have taken responsibility for myself and
protected myself instead of blaming it all on Arnez as if
he was the only reason I ended up with AIDS. The car
accident was not part of the plan though, and I didn't
plan for you to have to deal with your friend's death.
On a lighter note, congratulations on graduating and I
hope you become the best lawyer you possibly can. Be
safe.

I love you,
Cherese

Folding the paper into threes, I put it in the envelope
I'd been playing with, and lifted the handle of my suitcase.

Glancing at the table again, I picked up the brochure underneath it that I'd gotten from the clinic when I was tested. Walking out the door, I headed to the train. On my way there, I stopped in a mailing center to ship my letter for next-day delivery. When the clerk reached her hand out to take the envelope from me, I yanked it back and scratched my mother's apartment return address off. I handed the envelope back to her with my new address, the one that had a shelter for people like me. Black women who were 70% of all newly-diagnosed HIV positive patients.

Chapter 25: Memo

I closed my eyes and inhaled the incredible taste of tobacco. I'd quit smoking last semester but after the news Red told me about Cherese, I bought a pack on the way back to my place to pack clothes. In the car, when I told Jermaine the story, he was quiet. I didn't figure him to be as livid as I was about what Cherese did, but the way he sat nonchalantly in my car with his head against the window, I had to see what was on his mind.

"You know, it's not that I don't want to be mad about what happened to Arnez. But, at the same time, I can't say I lost a friend. A friend wouldn't let me marry a woman he got pregnant and not give him the opportunity to decide whether he wanted to father somebody else's baby. A friend wouldn't risk letting my fiancée get the disease he had."

"How do you know he knew he had it?"

Jermaine told me about a conversation he had with Anita and then with Arnez. I nodded my head and kept on driving. After I hit up the drugstore to buy more cigarettes, I drove back to my house. He told me about how Arnez looked so uncomfortable when the topic was brought up, and the more I listened, the more believable it was that he'd do that. But I still didn't understand his link to Cherese. When Arnez and I went to see Cherese the next day after the party she'd come to in Chicago, I introduced the two. He didn't know who she was and she didn't know who he was, so what beef could they possibly have? At the time, he and I had a little beef because I was pursuing Seleste and he liked her. I stopped at a red light and looked over at Jermaine.

"Eh, let me ask you a question. If I'd have tried to get at Cara while I knew you liked her, and if Cherese came around, would you try to get at her?"

Jermaine looked at me curiously. "Where is this coming from?"

"Tell me your answer first, and I'll tell you where I'm going with the question."

Jermaine twisted his lips and pondered on it before answering. "Well, there's a difference between like and love, so you know, I really love Cara. If you tried to get at her and I loved her like I do now, yeah, I'd have a problem with that. Would I try to get with Cherese? No disrespect, but Cherese is fine as hell. Even at the party, I'd checked her out. But when I saw her staring at you the whole time, I didn't say anything to her."

"But let's just say you and I weren't cool. Let's just say Arnez didn't introduce us and we didn't start being friends. Would you try to get up with Cherese?"

"If we weren't friends, no doubt. I mean, if you ain't with her and I wasn't with Cara at the time, then Cherese is free bait. Anybody at that party could've gotten at her."

I pressed the escalator. "And anybody on campus could've gotten at her too. I always thought it was strange that she knew I was at that party. There are parties all over campus but she knew exactly which one I was at. How could she know that without someone telling her?"

"Who do you think told her?"

I looked over at Jermaine. "Better question is who do I think fucked her."

He didn't answer for a minute. "Hey Travis."

"Oh gawd, my real name. What are you about to tell me that I don't want to hear? Nobody but Cara calls me by my real name unless they're going to tell me something I don't want to know."

"If you want to go to the Bronx, I'll go with you. The money I got back from the wedding, I'll use to buy the plane tickets, but I can't let you go by yourself. Arnez is already gone. I don't want anybody else out of our crew to be gone too. We might not be brothers in the sense that Arnez and

I were, or the way you and Jeremiah are, but you know, I
got your back."

I sucked my teeth. "You knew about Cherese, didn't
you?"

He leaned his elbows against his knees and rubbed
his eyebrows. "I didn't know who it was, but yeah, I did
know it was someone. One of the bruhs asked Arnez to
bring a woman with him that night before the party. He
wouldn't bring Anita, but he did tell us he did something
with some girl he'd never seen on campus. You got to
remember though, Arnez didn't know Cherese was coming,
so he didn't know the connection between you two."

I nodded. "My mother told me she was coming
though. I didn't tell anybody but O. Remember? I was
trying to play it off like I was drunk?"

Jermaine laughed. "Yeah, I remember that. So you
did know before she got there?"

"Yeah, but I never could figure out how she knew
where I was. Now I know. Arnez had to have told her."

"And knowing Arnez, he probably got a piece before
he..." Jermaine paused. "I'm sorry. I guess that's
disrespectful to talk about your ex-girl like that, but..."

I waved my hand dismissively at him. "Please. Ole
girl had sex with my father. You want to talk about some
talk show shit. After that, I don't put anything past her. But
I know she didn't intend to kill him. Now that I do believe.
Red said that she sent this guy we know here to beat him
up, and that sounds like the type of thing Cherese would
do. But Cherese is not into shooting and killing and all that.
She froze up every time she saw this target on my wall
from this shooting range Terrell and I use to go to when I
was in high school. She just wouldn't do that. But I can't
even say I blame her for doing what she did and sending
Dos here. On the other hand, she could've been a woman
about it and just told me what was going on. And I still
can't believe she had sex with Terrell. Of all the men in the

world, she picked my father." The more I thought about it, the angrier I got. Jermaine was quiet once again. I guess he couldn't find a way to rationalize that one either. We pulled up in front of my apartment and got out of the car.

As we were climbing the stairs, Jermaine spoke up once again. "Memo?"

"What's up?" I unlocked the door and walked directly to my bedroom with him following me inside.

"I changed my mind."

"About what?"

"About the plane ticket."

I looked at him. "What do you mean? Why?" I pulled my suitcase from the closet and pulled a key out of the closet.

"What does that key go to?" he asked me.

I didn't answer. Instead I put it inside the zipper pocket of my luggage and walked back to the closet to start packing clothes.

"Look, if you go there to New York, and the dude who did this to Arnez is there, he's probably already on edge. Hell, your father is already all over the news so there's too much drama going on there now. What do you think is going to happen if you show up in the Bronx..."

"Brooklyn."

"Whatever. What do you think is going to happen if you show up in New York trying to shoot everybody up."

"Who says I was going to shoot anybody?"

"You just told me you had a target on your wall. Then you put some mysterious key in your bag. C'mon now, I'm not stupid. I grew up in the same type of neighborhood you probably did, minus the cop father, but I know the deal."

I threw some shoes in the bag. "What should I do then? Call the cops? Umm, no thanks." A minute or so later, Seleste came barreling through the door. Ironically after lecturing Seleste about locking doors, I'd been too distracted to lock my own. Cara came in a minute or so later looking a little tired. I was too busy trying to pack to pay attention to what those two had to say. Nobody was going to talk me out of handling business. Jermaine and I kept on debating, Seleste was trying to put her two cents in, and Cara stayed quiet. I glanced at her sitting at my desk, but kept on walking back and forth to pack. After awhile, Jermaine's voice sounded muffled and Seleste might as well have been invisible by the way I was blocking them out. But Cara started to catch my attention more. She went from leaning on my desk to laying her arms on my computer keys. I saw my screen blinking in and out from her laying on a button, and I stopped packing to take a better look at her.

"Cara, babe, what's wrong?" I asked. When she tried to respond, I saw her lean forward and darted over to catch her before she fell out of the chair. Seleste ran to my bathroom and grabbed a towel from my pantry closet. She came back and put it over Cara's head. Jermaine kneeled in front of her to look in her face, but I saw him look down and gasp.

"Hold her," he ordered before he ran to my bathroom to get a bigger towel to wrap around her waist. I looked to see what he was doing and saw a red spot in the middle of her pants. My eyes widened, and I grabbed my keys. A couple of minutes later, we were back in my car with her laying on Jermaine's lap in the backseat. As soon as we got to the same hospital that Arnez was sent to, the emergency room attendant wheeled her in. Jermaine put on the gloves and gown that they'd demanded he use and took off after the nurses.

Seleste sat in a chair in the waiting room, legs crossed, talking on her cell. I sat down next to her, listening to her talk about Cara. By the gist of the conversation, I could tell she was talking to someone named Cecil who wanted to fly up to see her. She discouraged him from doing so and told him she'd call him back to tell him the news. I looked at my own phone and saw several voicemail messages and missed calls from my mother and one from Tweet. I called my mother back to let her know what was going on, and she was relieved to find out that I hadn't left the city. She asked me to promise that I wouldn't. I looked over at Seleste, who had her arms folded and gazed at a wall, and promised my mother I wasn't going anywhere. After I got off the phone with my mother, I called the other godfather of Cara's child. When Cara, Colleen, and I were at the gravesite earlier that day with O, Cara told O and I that she'd really like it if we could be the godfather to her child. That's what Arnez would've wanted, was what she'd said. I'm sure it was. But, I also wanted to know why he'd never told me Cara was pregnant. I could see him not telling Jermaine, considering the circumstances with the three of them, but I didn't get why I was left out. I guess there was a lot about Arnez I didn't know. I left a message with O about where we were and told him to give me a call if he wanted a ride to the hospital.

When I hung up the phone, a nurse walked by me and stopped to check me out. "Nice suit," she said with a grin.

I looked down and realized I still hadn't changed out of my graduation clothes. "Thank you," I said to her and wrapped my arm around Seleste, who looked absently on.

I dozed off soon after, until Jermaine flopped down next to me. I jumped a little and asked him what time it was. Two hours had passed. I tapped Seleste, who opened her eyes groggily, looked around, and groaned when she realized where she was. We both looked at Jermaine and waited on him to talk.

He looked over at me and a weary smile spread his face. "Man, this is a graduation day nobody will forget," he said.

I rubbed my eyes. "Is she going to be okay?"

"I don't know. The doctor kicked me out of the room, but they said she just looks tired. Stress. I guess with all of the stuff going on, she just had enough. I want her to have my girl though."

Seleste leaned over me and said, "I do too. Dressing up a goddaughter will be so much fun. Can we go see her?"

"The doctor told me to let her get some rest. Maybe in a few hours we can go in, unless you want to leave."

I looked at Seleste, who was looking back at me. "I'm not going anywhere."

Chapter 26: Cara

I woke up with someone messing with my fingers. Assuming it was the nurses sticking yet another IV needle in my body, I kept my eyes closed. But whomever was touching my hand held it. I opened my eyes lazily and looked at Jermaine standing over me.

"Hey," I mumbled.

"Hey," he replied. He looked down at my hand and I did the same. I saw the engagement ring he'd given me back on my left hand. I looked from the ring and back to him. My eyelids kept closing involuntarily, but I was determined to stay awake. "I was just thinking that...you know, I know you see the ring on your finger. But, looking at you in this hospital is blowing me. I wish they'd hurry up and release you so you could go back to being crazy talkative Cara. Looking at you in this gown just isn't cool. But more importantly, you not being with me isn't cool. So, I was hoping that you'd consider the engagement again. I know what I said before about not trusting you and feeling betrayed and all that, but all of that went right down the drain looking at you right now."

I cleared my throat and fought my eyes open. "Where did the ring come from?" I whispered.

"I put it on my pinky. I hadn't taken it off. I couldn't. It just didn't feel right to do so that quickly."

"Jermaine, I'm sorry about..."

He shushed me. "What's done is done. Nobody can take that back. But within the past two months, I've learned that I can't control what happens. I can only learn from it. It never occurred to me that you could have a baby by someone other than me, but it is what it is. I don't mean to sound corny, but I want you back because I just can't see not being with you."

I tried to squeeze his hand. "Jermaine, the doctor came in while you were gone."

He nodded his head, waiting on me to continue.

"There is no baby."

His eyebrow lifted. "What do you mean there is no baby?"

"I lost it. When you left the room, the…" My eyes clouded over with tears falling on each side of my face. He rubbed my hand. "Do you still want to…to be with me anyway?"

"Hell yeah I still want to be with you anyway."

My chest hurt when I tried to laugh, but I did form a smile. "I love you," I said. I saw his lips moving and my eyelids closed again.

"I love you more now than I ever did before, girl," he said. I felt a kiss on my lips and him still holding my hand.

*   *   *

The next day I was released from the hospital. Seleste and Jermaine helped me get dressed and Memo waited in the lobby for us. I reached out to hug him, with Jermaine carrying me.

"You didn't leave," I said to Memo.

He shook his head. "Nah, I didn't leave. You kind of put a nail in my plan."

I pinched his cheek. "Good, you didn't need to be going there anyway to deal with that crazy girl."

"Yeah, that's what everybody is telling me. My mother called me to tell me she'd called the police on Cherese once again. I don't know what's going to happen with that, but I'll leave it be. It's messed up that Arnez couldn't live his last days without…" He looked at me. "I'm sorry. I shouldn't even be talking about this. How are you?"

I waved him off. "It's okay. I'll be all right. As long as your mother is going to be okay with all the stuff going on, then it ended well, you know."

We walked to Memo's car, and Jermaine sat me in the backseat. Scooting across, I positioned myself so my back rested against his chest. Seleste asked me if I was okay, and I nodded at her. Memo jumped in the front seat and on the way out of the parking lot, I said, "Memo, can we just make one stop?" When he said yes, I told him where I wanted to go. Seleste looked curiously at me but agreed to go too. Jermaine stiffened underneath me but didn't say a word. A half n' hour later, we pulled up in front of the black gate of the cemetery where Arnez was buried. Jermaine helped me out of the car, and we walked over to his site. Arnez didn't have a stone yet, but there were spray-painted flowers in his fraternity colors surrounded around the dirt. I stood over his grave with the other three.

"I have something to say," Seleste said. "Although I'm not really a religious person, I just want to thank whoever made it possible for us to grow together again. I thought our friendship was falling apart with all of the things going on, but we're going to be okay. So, I just think we should go around and talk about something we're thankful for."

"Are we going to sing Koombayah too?" Memo said.

"Smart ass," she said.

I leaned into Jermaine and laughed lightly. "Okay, Seleste, I'm with that. I'll start. I'm thankful that we got together, and I'm also thankful that I was pregnant. I know you all will think that's weird, but in the past, I wasn't really mature about having a child. But after this situation, I know that I really do want to be a mother. So..." I looked at Jermaine. "Hopefully you'll help me out with that when we get married." I waved my finger at Seleste and Memo, who smiled.

"That's cool. I'm thankful you two could work
through your issues. I'm going to be real thankful if you
and Jermaine can make a girl. You know I don't want kids
so I have to have some girl to dress up and give toys to,"
Seleste said.

"You don't want kids?" Memo asked Seleste.

"Hell no. Unless they start taking a new route out,
I'm never having kids," she responded.

"We'll talk about that later," Memo said to her.

"Ain't nothing to talk about. I'm never having kids."

"You say that now."

"I'll say that twenty years from now. You can bet
your money on it!"

"I bet twenty dollars you change your mind within the
next twenty years," Jermaine egged the debate on.

"If you got change for a twenty, I'll make a bet for
ten. You know I'm broke now that my internship is over,"
Seleste said, laughing.

"You know what I think is cool? We've been through
so much stuff and gone so many places, but we still came
right back where we were. Sometimes it's good for things
to stay the same," Jermaine said. "That's what I'm thankful
for. That we made that round trip." He looked at Memo.
"So from one future dad to another, what are you thankful
for?"

"Cut that out. No future dads over this way," Seleste
snapped.

"Moving on," I interrupted, seeing Seleste was
getting mad for real.

"I don't care if future mommy is mad," Jermaine said.

"You know what? I'm going to clock you upside your
head if you don't leave me alone," she said to Jermaine.

Memo squatted down and picked up a little bit of dirt,
letting it run through his fingers. "You know what I'm
thankful for?"

"What?" she asked him.

"I'm thankful to be alive and healthy," he said. "And that you all talked me out of going to New York because I wouldn't have come back alive."

Seleste nodded. "I'm thankful that you didn't go too."

"All right, guys, I hate to interrupt, but I need to sit down," I said. Memo stood up, and they all fussed over me. Walking back to the car, I turned to look over my shoulder one last time.

Epilogue

Terrell was sentenced to five years in jail with the opportunity to be released a year later for good behavior. A few months later though, because the government refuses to issue condoms to prisoners, he was raped in jail. Two other prisoners became HIV positive due to the rape and are now blaming Terrell for it. He'll be lucky to see tomorrow.

Cara and Jermaine got married in Atlanta that same summer at Cecil's church with just Seleste, Memo, O, and a few family members who received relief for Hurricane Katrina. Many family members were not there because of the government withholding money to fix their old neighborhoods. Cara's mother never showed up but she did send a greeting card wishing her the best of luck. Cara is now interested in going on a reality show, while Jermaine continues to deejay until they can move to Atlanta for her try-outs. She is elated that Jermaine wants to move to Atlanta, since she wants to be close to her family now that she's pregnant again. Her new due date is in August of 2008. She will be having a girl.

Seleste is a paralegal at a popular Chicago law office, and Memo is using his money with the parole staff to put himself through law school. Memo is hinting at having kids but has perfect calf muscles from ducking when Seleste tries to whop him upside the head for saying such a thing.

O transferred to a college in Atlanta after seeing how much fun it was there during Cara and Jermaine's wedding. Unfortunately, all of his credits didn't transfer with him, so he's still in school and will not be graduating in December of 2007.

The police could not find sufficient evidence to link Cherese to Arnez's car accident. She continues to live in the shelter for AIDS patients until her last days. Dos is still walking around selling drugs to kill his community and thinks he's the man, and Red is now his sidekick. Renee now speaks out at events on HIV/AIDS while she waits on the final papers from Terrell for their divorce. She pawned her wedding band and donated the money to an organization trying to find a cure.

The person reading this novel will hopefully end this book by getting tested today. AIDS isn't a game, but if it was, it would always win. Protect yourself.

Shamontiel L. Vaughn

198